The Savannah Stories

First Comes Love

J.L. LEMON

ISBN–13: 978-0-6151-6775-6

Published 2007 by Up At Midnight Publishing
www.geocities.com/upatmidnightpublishing

As always, for my family who inspire me and keep my spirit alive with hope. This book as well as all the others wouldn't be possible without your love and support. Thank you.

Other titles available in the Savannah Stories:

Families are like fudge —
mostly sweet with a few nuts.

- Author Unknown

1

To call Savannah Prince a white knuckle flier was like describing Krakatau's eruption as inconsequential. Everything, not just her knuckles, blanched pale as snow when the wheels left the ground – and that was after she consumed nearly two Valiums.

She'd spent the better part of one day either in the air or waiting to board a plane. The layover at DFW airport seemed endless. But upon hearing her flight number called for boarding, she'd kinda wished the layover lasted longer.

Now the small prop plane slowly descended toward a little, secluded looking airport. For the past several minutes, besides praying the flying tin can didn't plow into the ground, Savannah searched the landscape and found it, for lack of a better word, flat. Very flat. In fact, she dared say it was barren. Of course, it was the dead of winter. She saw few trees but plenty of ground which traveled until it met the horizon with no hills or shelter belts of trees to obscure the view of West Texas.

This was Ennis Rutherford's home like Georgia's was hers. It would be an interesting trip visiting the Rutherford family. Since boarding the plane in Atlanta, she wondered how sane this idea truly was. His family sounded considerably boisterous on the phone. Ennis had three brothers with him being next to the youngest. One brother was married. Every one of them – minus Ennis – lived within two miles of their mother's house. According to Ennis, Savannah would be staying at the ranch house with him and his mother. Still questioning her common sense, Savannah remembered Georgia's parting words at the airport that morning. "Love you, hon. Call me every day and good luck with all those men."

She reached for her bags and purse and followed her fellow passengers out of the plane and into the elements. The first thing she noticed about the Texas Panhandle was the wind. A bitter gust mercilessly bit through her flesh. Pulling her jacket tighter around her, Savannah filed down the stairs and into the terminal. One thing about Hartsfield – the planes debarked through an *indoor* tunnel but she'd never flown on a prop plane nor landed at such a small airport. She chalked it up to there being a first for everything. She'd brought a book to read on her journey but once she departed from the jet at DFW airport and caught a gander at the aircraft awaiting her, she pocketed the mystery novel and took another half a Valium instead. The intense claustrophobic inside her rioted a battle with her nerves from takeoff to landing. Now she had to find her partner in the middle of all the strangers lingering, waiting for their friend or loved one at the gate. She'd had plenty to be nervous over. Not only had she traversed half the country by air, but since she was "meeting the family", she knew what that probably meant in the Rutherford household. She could almost hear the aria of "Here Comes the Bride".

Climbing stairs to the second floor, she began her search for her partner's handsome friendly face. She had no success finding Ennis. *Well, he'd better be here because I'm officially lost...* She visually studied the men in the crowd, past all the ones wearing baseball caps and cowboy hats. Ennis was nowhere to be found. Not that she couldn't get her hands on a directory somewhere. In a town this size, the book couldn't amount to the colossal volume of Atlanta's. All she had to do was look up the name Rutherford and make a call. Ennis promised he'd pick her up, though. When he promised something, he followed through.

Reinforcing her hold on the bags, she sighed once reaching the top stair. Looking around again, she was surprised when someone tapped her on the shoulder, "Hey, sugar," a familiar voice greeted.

Savannah stopped and sat her luggage down, much to the aggravation of passengers behind her. Hearing Ennis's baritone voice was akin to a choir of angels. She instantly felt her heart settle into a slower, steadier rhythm, allowing her to draw a long, calming breath. When she turned, her partner smiled. His six foot two inch frame looked sexier than ever in the worn jeans, rust colored polo shirt and matching blazer. As he smiled, his dark eyes seemed to join the ride as he brought her into a bear hug.

Savannah gratefully returned the embrace, replying, "Hey, partner." His warm, secure hold encouraged thoughts of melting into his arms. Then the rasp of stubble surprised her as he planted a quick kiss on her unsuspecting lips. The briefness barely permitted time to respond, especially with the Valiums circulating in her system.

Ennis gave her another squeeze then released her to pick up her bags, "How was your flight?"

"Fine," she lied. Problem was Ennis's expression informed her he knew it was an outright lie. Still, she continued, "We had a longer layover in Dallas than I expected but it gave me an opportunity to eat a bite and pick up a few things."

Ennis chuckled at her statement, "You went shopping at DFW?"

She shrugged, "You do with what you got." She felt his hand settle at the small of her back and decided the feeling was really very nice. But Ennis *was* very nice or she wouldn't have agreed to visit him in his native digs. A cop – or rather *she* – rarely found a partner she felt that comfortable with.

"I figure I'd best warn you now," he mentioned somewhat hesitantly.

Savannah suddenly stopped. The pressure of his hand on her back solidified with the action, and she had to remind herself not to enjoy it *too* much. They'd been partners long enough she'd learned his mannerisms and inflections. His current inflection indicated she may be walking into trouble in the first degree.

Ennis laughed nervously, another warning flag. He circled to her front, his cheeks flushed with color, "It's my family. They're gregarious and very presumptuous. My mother's real excited about meeting you and my brothers, they're really... Mostly it's Bobbi who thinks–"

"They think we're getting married, don't they?" Savannah's words emerged accusingly. She told her sister it would happen. Nearly all Southern families worked the same way. The only requirements were an unmarried relative, another person of legal age (preferably of the opposite sex) and the aforementioned family.

"Don't they?" she repeated again. Her tone brought a few stares from passers-by but she handily ignored them. Instead, she zeroed in on Ennis who'd suddenly begun perspiring. He knew she'd take to marriage the way a goldfish would take to rooming with a cat. And if *Georgia* knew about this and set her up, God help her. Being sideswiped by Cupid's Arrow was not in Savannah's immediate future, at least not if she had a say in it. She liked Ennis enough, that wasn't the problem. She liked him so much it felt like a sin. God knew between his face, physique and personality, he represented the epitome of temptation. The problem was, they were professional partners and she was forced to remind herself of that way too often lately. Between her own attraction to him and now his family's assumptions, she again questioned her decision about coming to Texas.

Ennis backpedaled verbally as though sensing her desire to flee Texas either by plane, train or foot, "I'm not proposing to you. Not that I don't want to because, well–"

"You're digging yourself deeper, Rutherford. Stop now before you turn up in China."

Ennis took a deep breath. "Okay, you know how I feel about you. But my family seems to have the impression we're more than just partners on the job."

"Dude," a twenty-something guy resembling a beach bum interjected while strolling by, "you are *so* screwed."

Savannah's vision strayed to the spiked blond hair and pierced nose-ringed fellow. Guiding her blue eyes back to Ennis's brown ones, she inquired, "Exactly how did they get this impression?"

She saw him swallow hard. After a long moment, he chanced speaking, "I may have disclosed my interest in you in various phone conversations over the past several months."

"May have? Ennis, tell me you didn't vow to marry me or bring me home to your mama for her stamp of approval."

"Sugar, they're the ones talking marriage, not me. I only told them how much I liked you."

As entertaining as it was listening to him retreat on a subject she knew *damn well* he felt strongly about, she hadn't the strength to battle his entire family while they tried to fit her for a bridal gown.

She stood staring into his pleading eyes. He obviously felt bad for the upcoming barrage of questions and knowing looks she'd be subjected to. Savannah shook her head, "My gut is telling me to turn tail and run back home." She witnessed the pain in his expression and changed her mind, "But I won't." Then she added the stipulation, "But one mention of how many kids we're having and I'm outta there, hear me?"

2

While driving through town, Ennis chatted nervously with her, explaining who was who in his family and their personalities, "My oldest brother is Cal, then there's Dane and Jake. Ma named Jake after John Wayne's character in 'Big Jake'. Now Cal's married to Bobbi who's real keen on weddings. Besides Ma, she's the one you have to worry about. Cal and Bobbi have a boy, Monty, who's around Lindsey's age. He's gonna take to you the moment he sees you."

Now she *knew* his nerves were getting the best of him. First, she already knew the basics of his family since he spoke often of them. Second, he'd seen how most kids reacted to her and it wasn't with hugs and cuddles. "Kids don't 'take to me', Ennis. That's Georgia's bailiwick."

Ennis eased off the accelerator. Since they were still inside the city limits, she wondered what he was doing, especially on the interstate. She had to hand it to this moderate sized city. The traffic was a breeze compared to Atlanta. They'd barreled down the interstate at sixty mph with no real obstacles. This part of Texas had one thing over Atlanta. Their roads were straightforward, not a convoluted mass of highways and streets aptly nicknamed "Spaghetti Junction".

Ennis smiled easily at her, "I'm sorry, but isn't that you Lindsey clings to like a vine when Seth wants to leave? She loves Georgia but she loves and adores you. Monty doesn't stand a chance. *He* may ask you to marry him."

With a tiny smile, Savannah shook her head. Yes, he was more nervous than a cat in a roomful of rocking chairs.

They drove along the interstate until the only sights were cows and horses meandering in pastures. "Ma made us all dinner. She'll tell you the recipe is an heirloom from a hundred generations ago. Truth is, she found it on the internet so don't believe everything she says."

Savannah turned away from him, her smile in full bloom now. If anything, this vacation would give her different things to occupy her time…

The new Ford pickup – Dane's truck, she learned during their travels – turned onto a narrow dirt road. About a half a mile later they approached a large ranch house that sat in an expanse of acreage. One barn stood a ways in the pasture, another further in the distance. "You grew up here?" she asked, visibly stunned.

"Yep. Big, huh?"

"You are the master of understatement." She saw a tall, burly figure round the corner of the house to the porch.

"There's Dane, making sure his truck is still in one piece." Ennis sounded slightly annoyed at either Dane's distrust or his intrusion on their time together.

Savannah watched Dane lean against a post support and halfway expected the beam to splinter from the wide set of shoulders against it. The word imposing came to mind for Dane. His shoulders were broader than Ennis's but his hips and waist slim like his brother's. He was number two in the line of Rutherford boys and according to Ennis, was Savannah's age. From what she could tell the gene pool ran deep in his family for when Dane looked up, she stared straight at Ennis's twin. He plopped a black Stetson atop a thick crop of dark hair as the truck neared. Dane directed his vision at her, and she sensed more than a hint of rogue in him. Maybe it was because Ennis forewarned her of his older brother's flirtatious ways. Or maybe it was simply she felt him sizing her up.

Ennis slid out of the seat and rounded Savannah's side to help her out. She winked at him, "Chivalrous fellow these days, aren't we? Keeping up appearances?"

He blushed, "It's no secret I have the hots for you."

Before she could reply, Dane crashed their conversation, "This your Georgia Peach you've been yammerin' about?"

Savannah watched Ennis's reaction. She could tell he wanted to deck Dane for smart aleck comment, "Her name is Savannah and if you piss her off, I'll hurt you."

The corners of Dane's mouth curled just slightly, enough to let Savannah know he would thoroughly enjoy the next several days. He swiveled on the heel of one boot and knocked twice on the front door, "Ennis is back and he brought a girl with him," he hollered in a tuneful manner.

It took no longer than ten seconds for a whirlwind to strike. The door flew open and three faces crowded the doorway. Savannah assumed they were Cal, his wife Bobbi, and Ennis's mother. They all appeared pleasant enough, excluding the eagerness brightening their features. Cal, the oldest brother, also favored Ennis. Savannah supposed this was Ennis in nine years. If so, he'd be equally as gorgeous at thirty-six as twenty-seven.

Mama Rutherford was the family glue, according to Ennis. She brought the family together for regular meals while attending to matters, both personal and business. Ennis compared her to Ellie Ewing of "Dallas" fame, family matriarch, mother, referee and priest all in one. She sure looked like she held her own, Savannah thought. Mama was short and plump but not in the neighborhood of fat. Judging by her size, Savannah wondered how the woman survived giving birth to men the sheer size of her boys. Few wrinkles creased Mama's friendly face but her elegantly styled hair – eerily reminiscent of Ellie Ewing's – was generously streaked with silver. The grin adorning her face spoke volumes and the first page read "Wedding Invitations". Much as Savannah enjoyed the show, she really had no interest in getting hitched at Southfork.

Bobbi concerned her most. The trim redhead looked capable of planning anything, from the D-Day invasion to a surprise wedding. A heavy dash of resourcefulness flavored the woman's features giving Savannah the heebies before even stepping foot in the house. Of course she also attributed Bobbi's knowing smile, a greeting that basically screamed "Welcome to the family", for a lot of the uneasiness.

Savannah felt herself gradually backpedal – right against Ennis's chest. His hand went on her hip, "There, there," he tried to settle her. "Before you run away, you have to eat. Ma won't let anyone go hungry."

"It isn't 'Ma' I'm worried about," she whispered back. "It's your sister-in-law."

Ennis couldn't help but chuckle, "She shouldn't bite but if she does, she's had her shots." He unloaded her suitcases and eased his arm around her, "Everybody, this is my partner Savannah Prince."

"Hello, Savannah," they all greeted in unison, their grins still gnawing at her quickly fraying nerves. This had to be a set-up of some kind. They looked too damned happy.

She smiled back, returning their salutation. Ennis began introductions – a formality since she'd already pegged who was who. Suddenly a little face appeared from behind Bobbi. Savannah knew instantly it was Monty. Ennis proudly displayed photos of him in his wallet like she kept photos of Lindsey and Dylan in her purse. Monty sported the "Rutherford" features from his dark, unruly hair, his nose and slant of his wily grin. He inherited only one characteristic from Bobbi: blue eyes. Savannah mulled over the last point. If the men's genes held that potency, God help the women who married them. No one would see the mother's resemblance in the baby at all.

A lock of the boy's hair fell askew across his forehead in a cute manner. A hint of shyness mixed with cunning flavored his expression as he clung to his mother. He stared at Savannah, his blue eyes shining then he whispered to his mother, "Is that Uncle Ennis's girlfriend?"

Unfortunately, as Bobbi sat a hand on his shoulder, she nodded,

"M-hmm. Her name is Savannah. Go say hi to her and remember your manners."

Savannah watched the young boy's hands fidget then finally slide into his jeans pockets as he neared. For some reason, his nervousness seemed as palpable as hers. The least she could do was ease his concern about her so she dipped to one knee and broke the ice, "You must be Monty."

The boy refused to meet her gaze but nodded shyly while toeing the ground. Savannah continued, "I've heard a lot about you. Ennis thinks you're about the greatest nephew around."

With pure admiration, Monty's vision swung up to Ennis who winked. The comment seemed to relax him and the boy thrust his hand out to her, "He likes you too. A lot."

Savannah wrapped her hand around his and unexpectedly, he shifted his gaze to her as she spoke, "So I've heard."

"You talk funny."

"Montgomery!" Bobbi scolded and started toward her son. Waving her off, Savannah chuckled softly, "I suppose to most Texans I do talk funny. You see, I'm from Georgia. Do you know where that is?"

The boy kept a hold on her hand and nodded bashfully. She continued, "Maybe someday you'll come visit and if you do, I know all the fun places to go."

3

The cyclone aptly named the Rutherford family hit with a vengeance. She fielded questions about herself, her life in Atlanta, and hers and Ennis's relationship until her voice threatened to give out. They sat down to eat but the family managed to all consume food while the others lobbed questions like hand grenades. She'd barely cleaned her plate when her cell phone rang. The brood— minus Jake – finally let her catch her breath. Savannah wanted to speak to her sister alone however it was not permitted between all interested parties still staring a gaping hole in her. "Prince," she practically squeaked into the receiver. Georgia immediately turned Mother Hen on her, politely demanding to know why she hadn't called when the plane landed. Savannah attempted to explain in a diplomatic way that she'd been "lavished" in attention from the moment she arrived. Actually, she'd been smothered in it with no room to come up for air. Georgia reminded her of the cookies she'd sent and Savannah promised to present them immediately after their conversation – or sooner if possible.

"The candy cane cookies are for –"

"I know," Savannah said. "The candy cane cookies are for

Monty. Listen, I'll call you later, okay? It's kinda busy right now."

They'd ended the conversation and that sent Monty into a feverish chant for cookies. Savannah searched one of the bags she brought and finally – to her great relief – discovered the Tupperware containers filled to the brim with goodies. "My sister made these. The pecan praline cookies are made from my grandmother's recipe. And these," she handed the candy cane cookies to Monty, "are for you. My niece and nephew demand them at Christmas every year." She watched the young boy latch onto the container with an enthusiasm seen only in Lindsey and Dylan. He whispered a bashful "thanks" and ran off.

She stood up to stretch her legs, "I brought gifts so I think I'll go place them under the tree." She carried the bag into the living room. The family decorated the house early for Christmas. Only about a month early, she thought to herself. She'd spent Thanksgiving with Georgia and Seth then two days later she boarded the plane to Texas. This holiday season was one for the record books already.

The entire ranch house dripped with Christmas cheer, from window decorations to garland draped as far as the eye could see. Mama Rutherford even hung mistletoe in the entry into the living room. Besides the kitchen, that particular area appeared designated the Christmas room. She marveled at the miniature Santa standing only knee high, not to mention the little reindeer whose nose glowed red and head raised and lowered like he was eating.

She approached the Christmas tree which she soon discovered was real. Far from the plastic things she grew up with and Georgia and Seth still assembled to this day. Savannah always thought real trees were better, plus they didn't provide the unconditional aggravation of putting one together. She couldn't resist lifting a bough to her nose and breathing in the rich pine smell.

The Rutherfords trimmed their Christmas tree in a boatload of multicolored lights that winked at alternate times. They wrapped gold tinsel around the tree and hung western type ornaments on the branches. She saw carefully painted ceramic boots, cowboy hats, saddles and horses gracing the limbs. Closer to the bottom she spied a few homemade ornaments, probably Monty's work at school. One looked suspiciously like a longhorn cow with one broken horn.

Savannah began unloading one of the smaller suitcases she'd brought along. With Ennis's help, she'd chosen gifts for each of his relatives. He gave her hints of everyone's preferences, allowing her to make the final decision. Monty was possibly the easiest to buy for since he followed the majority of young boys in Texas. He loved the Dallas Cowboys. Living in Atlanta and searching for Cowboy merchandise proved to be a veritable nightmare. She'd ended up ordering that gift on the internet.

"You know, you didn't have to bring us gifts, Peach. We'd have liked you either way."

She now recognized Dane without glancing back. Concluding her Santa duty, she closed the suitcase and rose to her feet. He finished chewing a pecan praline cookie, swallowed then threw another in his mouth, "Your sister married?"

"Yes, she is. To a marine."

He nodded, "He deployed?"

When she herself nodded in response, his brow sank, "Shame. He's missin' out on all this great cookin'."

"She loves to cook. Guess that's why she's good at it." She noticed he had a penchant for leaning. Give Dane a wall and he was happy as a clam, obviously. He chewed thoughtfully, his dark eyes trained on her, "Your sister look anything like you?"

She wasn't stupid enough to explain that of the two sisters, Savannah was the homelier one and that Georgia was Rita Hayworth reincarnated. All her life she heard how "beautiful" Georgia was and how "cute" Savannah was. The needle on the jealousy scale bumped only occasionally. Savannah knew beauty could be its own curse. She was merely happy to inherit what she had from Charlene and the Culberson side.

Dane surprised her by answering his own question, "Ennis says she's pretty but nothing like you." He leaned a tad closer, "He called you a knockout and I wholeheartedly agree."

She felt a blush heat her face and she thanked him. Savannah migrated to the loveseat, hoping Ennis might appear soon. Instead, Dane shrugged his weight back to both feet and settled next to her, "You know, you're the first woman Ennis has ever brought home."

She liked Dane okay. He reminded her a bit of herself. She'd given Georgia hell over boyfriends she brought home and even managed to aggravate the young men in the process. What she didn't appreciate was being on the receiving end of the treatment.

Savannah lifted her chin, meeting his gaze, "Is this a good or bad thing?"

His eyes revealed the joy in their bantering, "Understand this is strictly my opinion but I'd say it's a good thing for him and a bad one for you."

Savannah laughed easily. Dane's head tilted slightly as if to savor the sound. It took a moment for her to recover, "Why would you say that? Don't you love your brother?"

"Sure, I do," he agreed. "But you don't know all his bad habits. They'll drive you silly."

"We've been partners long enough I can order his coffee or his hamburger the way he likes it. He can do the same for me. I haven't noticed very many bad habits with the distinct exception of him occasionally skimping on cream in my coffee." She winked at him, "I think I can overlook that."

She figured Dane was trying to one, make her feel very uncomfortable in his own odd way or two, trying to make her feel comfortable and failing miserably. She preferred to believe the latter.

"Savannah's a weird name." The statement came as a surprise but thankfully it didn't come from Dane's lips. She turned in the direction of the voice to see Monty standing, a suspicious frown on his kid face. As she absorbed the declaration, she watched an overstuffed pillow bean the child in the face, knocking him back a step. "Hey," Dane grabbed another pillow, "where are your manners?"

Savannah stopped him with a hand on his arm. When their vision met, she noticed Dane stared at her. His chin twitched slightly as though something fought to escape his closed lips.

Savannah offered, "It is an unusual name, Monty's right." She waved the boy to her. Cautiously he approached much like he might a large unfamiliar dog. She patted the loveseat between her and Dane. Monty piled up between them, leaning into Dane's chest. The older Rutherford scrubbed his knuckles against the boy's head good-naturedly, "Apologize to her. I think Savannah's a pretty name, not weird at all."

Realizing his blunder, Monty puffed his lower lip, "Sorry, Savannah."

"That's okay. It's not a name you hear every day, I know."

"Kids at school think my name's weird."

"It's not either," she assured. "I like your name."

"Yeah," Dane added, "you were named after your grandpa." He looked at Savannah, "She was probably named after her ma."

She nodded, "My middle name, yes. They named me Savannah because they honeymooned there." She could have dropkicked herself through the goalposts at Texas Stadium for volunteering that. Of all the things to say – honeymoon.

"Hey, everyone's making off with my partner but me," Ennis's voice entered from behind.

Monty climbed down from Dane's lap and ran into the kitchen, leaving the three adults to talk. Dane patted her arm, "Best keep a close eye on this gal. All the single fellas will be after her."

Ennis stared balefully at Dane's hand, "Does that include my brothers?"

Her stomach twisted but she fended off any outward signs of unease. Their exchange plainly exposed raw feelings between the brothers. Feelings Ennis hadn't informed her about previously. She hoped that was the only surprise awaiting her because she hadn't planned on navigating a mine field during her visit.

Ennis pushed Dane's feet aside with his own then proceeded to sit between his brother and Savannah. He wriggled backward until he decidedly separated the two. Dane threw him a sharp glance and voiced his aggravation, "Geez, Ennis. From now on, take out an ad saying 'I'm the most insecure man in the family.'"

"There's plenty of room on this couch," Ennis retorted gruffly.

"It's a *loveseat*, moron. Made for two people, not three."

Their antics caused Savannah to curb a smile. Ennis hadn't anything to worry about but evidenced by his threatening scowl, he clearly didn't believe it. Judging by Dane's reaction, he realized his brother's seriousness, especially when Ennis added with a degree of finality, "Then find another chair."

Shaking his head, Dane snorted, "Oh, is it the 'I brung her to the dance' song?"

Savannah couldn't stop from chuckling now. The sound bubbled out, catching both men's attention. Dane smiled what she considered a cautionary smile, "You're laughing now, honey, but I've never seen my brother so silly over a woman. You'd best keep your bloomers drawn tight." He bowed to Ennis, "I'm fetching some chocolate pie. That okay with you, sire?"

"Get outta here before I slug you," Ennis mumbled, his hand moving to Savannah's knee. She didn't remove it however she realized Dane was correct. Ennis felt threatened and with the house full of mostly single men, she could see why. A new face around the house could instill fear in the most confident person.

Before rising, Dane lifted his gaze to Savannah, "Bring you anything to eat, honey?"

She shook her head and thanked him. Ennis's grasp on her knee tightened slightly and she covered his hand with hers, giving it a reassuring squeeze, "Calm down. He's just being nice."

He looked after Dane, ensuring he didn't deviate from his objective. His brother picked up a saucer and purposefully waved the fork at Ennis. Now Ennis calmed a bit, his voice low, "No, he's not just being nice."

"He said I'm the first woman you've brought home –"

"The first one he hadn't pilfered from me, you mean. He's lifted every girlfriend I've ever had."

"Ennis Rutherford," she teased, "you're afraid I'll succumb to your brother's charms?"

He didn't readily answer her. His hand squeezed hers and he softened his voice even more, "I'd rather you succumb to mine."

4

He'd brooded and brooded since the confrontation with Dane, she noticed. The stress poured from him and strangely, she picked up on it. After everyone ate their fill of dessert – Savannah indulged in a slice of pecan pie, complete with a dollop of ice cream courtesy of Ennis – they all settled in for the evening. So it shocked Savannah when Ennis gathered their suitcases into Dane's truck. Evidently it hit the rest of the family the same way. "I thought y'all were staying here," Dane reminded. His tone and stance screamed his annoyance to Ennis's joy.

"Nope. We're staying at the ranch house."

"We are?" Savannah inquired, just as surprised at the change.

"Uh, Ennis," Bobbi interjected softly, "why don't we leave the arrangements as is?"

He rotated on his heel, his reply as calm as hers, "Because she's used to me and my peculiarities but knowing my brothers," he threw a heated glare at Dane, "they'll scare her off and I'll find her at the airport begging to go home."

Dane laughed which inspired a smile from Savannah. She'd never seen Ennis display such a possessive streak. Mama Rutherford, listening to the conversation, dried her hands on a dishtowel and presented her best parental frown, "You think traipsing her off to the ranch house will prevent your brothers from interacting with her?"

Ennis bit the inside of his jaw. Savannah recognized the move when he wanted to say something so bad, he bit his jaw instead. Mama Rutherford continued, her vision on her son, "I know you're both old enough to make your own decisions but stashing her away won't work, not with your brothers. Plus, it's not wise for the two of you to be under the same roof alone. Savannah knows what I mean, don't you, honey?"

Savannah's mouth opened to reply but Ennis cut her off, "God sakes, Ma. We're not living in the 1800's–"

A new voice added to the mix, "If they want to romp at the ranch house, let 'em. Least it'll keep it quiet here."

Savannah flinched with the statement and Ennis saw it. Her reaction drove his temper into overdrive and he shouldered past Dane. The next thing Savannah heard was a solid thud and pictures rattling on the wall. "You little punk," Ennis growled. "I'm still big enough to kick your scrawny ass so you apologize to Savannah right now."

A scuffle of feet drew Dane up short and he stepped aside for Ennis, fists wrapped in Jake's shirt, to haul his brother to face Savannah.

She, on the other hand, was entertaining the return to Atlanta as stated earlier. But, at the current time, she was face to face with a lumberjack who hadn't shaved in a few days. A lumberjack with the same unruly dark hair and grin she'd seen so often on her partner. The Rutherford genes rivaled the Kennedy's for producing boys that strongly favored one another.

Jake's grin widened, "Hey, she's not ugly. Ennis said the girls in Georgia were uglier than homemade soap but this one's cute as a speckled pup."

Even as Ennis's temper visibly percolated, Jake's brow bobbed up and down suggestively at Savannah, "Hiya, sweetheart."

It was, at that point, she decided Ennis's family was crazier than hers – and that definitely took work. While her expression never changed, her inner temperature gauge fluttered close to red. She would not lose her temper, not in front of Ennis and his family. She would, though, discreetly find a way to return home – if things didn't settle down fast.

When Ennis heard Jake's "greeting", he rammed him against the wall again. This time Savannah calmly approached and placed a gentle hand on his arm, "Ennis, let him go."

Her voice broke his intense glare at his brother and he looked at his partner, his cheeks flaming crimson, "Not before teaching him a lesson about respect."

Before Savannah could say another word, Mama Rutherford smacked Ennis's bottom with a dishtowel, "I'll teach you both about it. Now let your brother go."

The moment he released Jake, their mother whacked Jake across the hip with the towel, "An' you, young man, apologize to Savannah. I'm sick an' tired of this family showing its bad side to her."

"You mean its 'back side', don't you, Ma?" Dane interjected while giving Savannah a wink.

"That too." She heaved a sigh, "Good Lord, you'd think we'd

never had company the way you boys are acting. Only decent one is Cal."

Bobbi offered an explanation, "That's because he's been gawking over pretty girls since junior high. He's now perfected it into a silent admiration."

Jake belly-laughed, "Nothing to do with the fact you'd slam an iron skillet 'cross his nose if he *spoke* an 'admiring' word to her."

"I'll slam one 'cross yours, Jacob Rutherford," she replied. With her tone, Savannah suspected Bobbi meant it too.

"Everyone shut up," Ennis ordered in a voice his partner never heard before. Even she, without speaking, clammed up a little tighter. He slid his arm around her shoulders, "You're all acting like nitwits and I can already feel Savannah dialing her sister and telling her to meet her at the airport."

Good call, Savannah thought. Because that was *precisely* what she was thinking. At that announcement, the Rutherford family suddenly began closing in on her, the women contrite, the men displaying friendly yet slightly rapacious grins. Again, Ennis came to the rescue, "Oh no, you don't. Give her space, in fact, give us both some." He guided her by the shoulders into the living room where he hefted her last suitcase into his free hand. Monty peeked out from behind the baby grand piano in the corner. Ennis spied him and waved him over, "Grab that other bag, will ya, Monty? Thanks."

He steered her out the door and into the pickup. After loading their bags, he faced his family who'd followed behind like whipped puppies, "Look, we're used to each other's ways, Savannah's not. This is like dumping her in the middle of a gunfight unarmed. We'll stay at the ranch house," he glanced at his mother, "together. We're adults but we're not stupid so there's no need for a chaperone."

5

Savannah let Ennis cool down the better part of thirty minutes, allowing him to unload the truck (he refused to let her help) and then show her around the quaint ranch house. Equipped like a modern apartment, the house was small with one main room with the kitchen on one side and the bed and couch on the other. The bathroom was tucked off to the side, the only room with a door for privacy. For a couple starting out, it was perfect – which was something not lost on her. The Rutherford Ranch had four houses on it: the main house, the little ranch house, and at the back of the land were Cal and Bobbi's place then another, smaller house for Dane. Jake still resided at the main house.

Mama Rutherford was no fool, Savannah sensed that from the get-go. Judging by the fresh linens on the bed and the well stocked pantry and cabinets, the older woman expected the two to retire to the little ranch house for privacy. But like all good mothers, she put up a customary and convincing fuss about the two being alone. The thought brought a gentle smile to Savannah. At least Mama could say she tried.

The Little Ranch House Built for Two contained heavy oak furniture – from the chairs and bed, all the way to the kitchen cabinets, chest of drawers and nightstand beside the bed. A tornado might sweep the house away but she'd bet a hundred bucks the furniture stayed in place, not moving an inch. Looking around, Savannah felt the warmth of the house with its cross-stitched Bible verses hanging on the walls. A smile crossed her face at the large John Wayne portrait hanging next to the front door. It was, appropriately, from the movie "Big Jake".

While they had traveled the dusty road to the ranch house, Savannah listened to Ennis explain that the "ranch" was mostly farmland but as a tradeoff to his father, Mama Rutherford insisted on her share of animals as well. They had cows, horses, hogs and chickens "out that way" he pointed. Savannah saw several small buildings, she assumed, serving as stables and pens for most of them. Along the way, however, she noticed several Hereford cows dispersed among the land.

Now she stood, staring out the kitchen's blue lace trimmed curtains at cows wandering around the pasture. Cows were bigger than she imagined. For some reason, she figured them to be short, maybe to her elbows. She hadn't expected them to stand practically to her neck.

"Savannah?"

The calling of her name broke her daze and she looked toward Ennis, "Sorry. I was just thinking."

"Yeah, about how nutty my family is." He neared her and kissed her cheek, "I'm sorry about all that. I was afraid they'd go stupid on me. Anytime one of us brings in a girl, that's all it takes."

"Ennis, don't apologize. They're doing the same thing I did to Georgia when she'd bring home a boy."

His palm cupped her cheek, "That's just being a naughty kid.

They, on the other hand, are being criminal."

Savannah wasn't sure what he meant. Ennis saw her confusion and his large hand curled behind her neck, the fingertips tenderly rubbing the tension away. She felt herself instantly relax while he explained, "My brothers think you're the cat's meow, sugar, and they're not above trying to sneak a lap of milk."

"For that to happen, I'd have to give permission," she basically moaned. "I don't see it happening in the near future." She noticed how touchy-feely her partner became since she arrived. Normally, he kept to himself with the exception of a kiss here and there or a brush of his hand on her back. She certainly never objected and now since he started touching her more intimately, she didn't plan on interrupting him at this point either. Ennis possessed a gift of touch she'd never experienced.

His fingers continued their massage, and his other arm curled around her waist, drawing her closer, "Clarify 'the near future' for me."

Her eyes drifted closed, "Oh, the next millennium or so." She heard Ennis chuckle but she was too busy melting into his embrace. "Ennis," she moaned, not wanting to allow herself this indulgence but doing it anyway.

"M-hmm?" his voice dropped to a low, sexy rumble. Damn it, he *knew* she enjoyed his touch. He probably also knew how much.

Savannah pressed her cheek against his broad chest and found herself holding to him just to keep her bearings. Her partner held her securely in his arms. Sighing from the tender massage, she asked, "Did you put something in my tea?"

His gentle laughter sounded like soft thunder in her ear, "I'll never tell." Ennis moved from her neck to pet her hair slowly, reverently. After a hesitant moment, he dipped a toe into unknown waters, "Holding you like this sure does feel fine."

Before giving herself time to think, she replied, "Yes, it does."

"Savannah, I want to say –" he began when the phone cut off his declaration. He muttered an expletive under his breath.

She started withdrawing from his hold and felt him resist the move. He'd settled into their embrace with the obvious intention of keeping it a while. But, realizing the phone wouldn't cease the incessant ringing, he let her break the hug while he stomped to the jangling bugger and ripped it savagely from its cradle, "What?"

Savannah giggled almost silently. Ennis was most definitely ready to hurt someone related to him – either Jake or Dane. On the other hand, she learned she was wrong.

"Yes, Ma. I'm just getting her settled, showing her around. Yes, we have enough blankets. No, Ma, I know Savannah gets the bed and I take the couch. I haven't lost *my* manners unlike my brothers. The cupboards are stocked, I already checked." He glanced at Savannah as if begging for help, "If we need anything just come to the house. Okay, thanks, Ma… Right, I'll ask." He now focused directly on his partner and decisively shook his head, "Do you want to join everyone for breakfast in the morning?" He must have sensed Savannah's reply because he pointedly turned his back to her, "Uh, Ma? She's pretty worn out. We'll just grab a bite here and head out to the house later. Maybe spend some alone time with you, what about that?" He turned back to Savannah and nodded, "Okay, we'll see you then. Love you too."

When he hung up the phone, Savannah batted her eyes innocently, "Why don't you want to have breakfast with everyone?"

Ennis caught her inflection and met it with a mischievous grin, "'Cause the only lair you should be in is mine, not theirs." He stepped closer to her and she lifted her vision to his, "Ennis, what were you saying before the phone rang?"

Now he faltered, she noticed. His courage wilted for some reason, probably his mother's phone call. He reached forward, twirling a lock of her hair around his finger, "I was saying I'm glad you came."

That wasn't what he planned to say earlier. Savannah knew it. He'd built up for that one, like it took every cell in his body to gather the guts to broach the subject – this thinly veiled replacement, while heartwarming, just didn't support that garnering of courage.

She smiled into his handsome features, and decided not to further her thought, "I am too."

Ennis couldn't believe his mother's timing. Here he tried to express his true feelings for Savannah – if even in a small way – and his family torpedoed the effort. He hadn't anticipated the outright barrage his brothers subjected her to. What impressed him was her ability to remain calm under fire. It only deepened his affection for her. He knew she was cool under fire at work but to take on his brother's frontal assault so gracefully told him a lot about his partner.

He thought back to the moment he saw her climb down the stairs of the plane. To others, she probably appeared cool and collected. Ennis knew better. He realized the Olympic effort it took for her to board a small aircraft and retain that degree of decorum. Besides her siblings, he was the only person to grasp the depth of her fear. Shortly after they partnered he discovered she suffered from clinical claustrophobia. To her, flying in a plane equated to throwing a quadriplegic into a pool and saying "swim". At best, they'd survive because they relaxed and floated. On the way home, Savannah admitted to taking a Valium in Atlanta and another half a pill in Dallas. By the time the plane landed, Ennis would've sworn she'd flown stone sober and not a tranquilizer to her name. Her eyes always gave her away. Their scarcely restrained panic twisted his heart. She'd endured a living hell to come see him.

Ever since they met, his blood roared in his veins anytime he thought of her or saw her. Her beautiful face had features reminding him of Rita Hayworth. Even her long chestnut waves were reminiscent of the movie star's. She looked like every man's fantasy and she couldn't understand his concern about Dane muscling in. It completely amazed him...

He glanced toward the bathroom where Savannah retreated to shower and change for bed. Suddenly he realized why his mother's face froze in stark terror at the idea of them staying together. His hunger for Savannah Prince verged on starvation. The pitter-patter of water told Ennis she was rinsing. Mentally, he followed her hands as they roamed in places his fingers ached to touch, to stroke... Ennis licked his lips and cringed at his body's reaction. He could nearly feel the phone ring – somehow his family had telepathy. They sensed his body's desire for her.

Ennis leaned across the bed and yanked the phone plug free from the wall. No, they weren't interrupting him this time. He wanted time alone with Savannah, to talk personally, to kiss her, to feel what he'd been dreaming of for a year now. He wouldn't force her to do anything except listen to him. She'd do that, he knew, but he also recognized the challenge he faced. He couldn't tell her he loved her yet. That would scare her off. She'd made it perfectly clear since Day One that getting married was for other women.

The bathroom door opened and Savannah startled slightly at the sight of Ennis sitting on the bed. "Hi," was the awkward salutation.

"Hi," he answered deep and rough. Inwardly, he panicked, horrified that his desire spoke so clearly. He scrambled to fix his voice, "Thought I'd stick around and offer..." his mind suddenly went blank. She stepped into the room, her long, damp waves cascading down her shoulders. Her purple silk pajamas highlighted her trim figure and those lovely breasts that caused him so many sleepless nights. The cool air tightened her nipples, inviting his tongue and teeth to try them out.

"Offer what?" she softly reminded him, attempting to refocus his attention.

His hands lifted slightly, the fingers waving absently in the air, "Um," was all he managed. *Uh-oh...*

She began walking toward him, her breasts swaying gently with the motion. He was doomed, literally doomed, his mind screamed. Now she stood directly in front of him, her hand cupped his chin and lifted his vision from her breasts, "Ennis, what were you offering?"

"Massage," he blurted then grinned like a blushing, lovesick schoolboy. He stole a brief glance at her right breast then raced back to her sparkling blue eyes. She smelled like a field of flowers. The delicate scent wafting into his nostrils caused his arousal to threaten a jail break. His pants tightened to painful proportions and he flinched slightly.

The corners of Savannah's mouth rose in a small smile, "What kind of massage?"

Impulse instructed him to plant his hands on the objects of his obsession and show her. Common sense ordered him to plant his hands on her hips and behave.

It took every ounce of self-control to do the latter, but he did. His fingers rubbed at the base of her spine, content to feel her warmth through the silk. Moving northward, his fingertips massaged deeper, slower.

Savannah's eyes closed and she moaned softly. The sound tightened his groin and loosened his resolve. If she moaned like that over a momentary massage, how would she sound during an extended stretch of lovemaking? *Down boy*, he told himself. But when her hands rested on his shoulders which inadvertently drew her breasts closer, everything went *up* and in very painful proportions.

Ennis had to squeeze the words out with some semblance of composure, "You interested in my offer?"

Her eyes opened even as his fingertips danced in relaxing circles across her lower back, "You're not jeopardizing my reputation are you, Mr. Rutherford?"

He couldn't help but smile at her deep Southern drawl, hugely exaggerated for the question. She'd sounded more like her sister with the thick brogue rather than Savannah with a lighter accent to her speech.

Ennis barely shook his head, "Not yet, Miss Prince, but give me some time and I'll work on it."

Her low, sonorous laugh heightened his need and the pitch in his jeans. When she ran her fingers through his hair, he swore the denim would strangle his manhood. Either way, Savannah would be the death of him if he didn't have her all to his own forever. Her voice returned to its normal effortless drawl, "Your mother would have a conniption if she caught us like this, much less if we were horizontal."

No shit, he agreed silently. "She can have a conniption and my brothers can have stone aches for all I care right now. I just want us to have time together and I want to give you a massage. You've had a rough day and need to relax."

Savannah looked skeptical at his reasoning. One brow dipped while the other lifted somewhat, "That the only reason?"

He slid his hands around her waist, his thumbs lightly stroked her stomach. He liked her expression when he did it. A combination of brief surprise followed closely by acquiescence to his touch. He dipped an index finger into her navel, bringing her eyes open again.

"You know that's not the only reason," he said. "I've wanted to get my hands on you since the day we met and if you agree, I'll finally get my wish." When her mouth opened to speak, he feared a rejection so he began stroking her stomach ever-so-lightly again.

The motion had her gradually falling under his spell once more and she moaned, "How's a girl supposed to think straight when you're doing that?"

Ennis felt a distinct sensation creeping into his brain.

Possessiveness. The longer he watched her react to his touch, the deeper it rooted itself, "Hopefully, she's not." His voice lowered to a whisper, "Hopefully, she won't resist my offer or my touch," he leaned forward and placed a gentle kiss to her navel, "or my kiss."

The sensation of his lips through the silk surprised her. She jerked slightly and glanced down in time to see him place another soft kiss in the same place. Ennis suppressed his own groan when her fingers sifted through his hair. They cupped the back of his head, tilting him back to meet her gaze, "Ennis,"

Uh-oh, his mind cringed. That didn't sound like a "take me now" ambiance in her tone. It was more the "not here, not now". He tenderly clasped her hips and attempted to regroup his poise, "I'm not asking for that, sugar. My aim right now is to give you a massage."

"You're giving me more than that, baby. I'm strong-willed but I'm still female."

I'm well aware of that last part. But she left the hint she might be open to his advances later. That thought made him smile. His fingertips tickled the small of her back, "Then my goal is to break your stubborn streak at some point." He drew one hand across the bed in an elaborate motion, "For now, please allow me to show you my other talents besides cuffing bad guys."

Her brow slanted in a humorous fashion, "As long as you don't intend to cuff *me*, we're all right."

Ennis's hard-on pulsed against his jeans. The mere idea of seeing her in that position, waiting for him, begging... He tore the thought from his mind as smoothly as ripping a needle from a record. At least his mouth worked better than his brain, "Sweetheart, when I break you, I won't need cuffs. You'll stay willingly."

Savannah, halfway in the reclining position, stopped. She regarded his statement carefully, "You're terribly confident this will happen."

Ennis, feeling he'd gained ground on his obstinate partner, eased her down by the shoulders, "Oh, it will. You're a smart dame. Only a matter of time until you realize we make a great team in more ways than one."

He felt her resist him a bit, her voice feigning insult, "Did you just call me a dame?"

He laughed, "Easy, sugar. At this rate you'll never get any sleep."

"With you hovering over me talking handcuffs and calling me a dame, you're right." She seemed to be partially bantering with him since she laid down flat after having her say.

Ennis decided to give her another shock and walked his fingers up her stomach, between her breasts and stopped, "You'd rather I massage your front and not your back?"

Savannah snorted at the question then flipped onto her stomach, "You're maddening, Ennis. Positively maddening."

He watched her situate herself before doing anything. She planted her chin on top of her crossed arms. Ennis smiled at the beauty splayed in front of him.

He ran a light touch up the back of her thigh that caused not only the muscle to twitch but brought a short gasp from her. He topped off the move with a mild swat to her bottom, "That's for calling me maddening."

Savannah twisted to see his sly grin and leveled a semi-serious glare at him, "Do that again and I promise a massage will be the last thing on your mind."

Her voice indicated absolute sternness. Her eyes, however, told a whole different story. He would heed the voice tonight, no matter what her eyes said. Ennis's fingers eased beneath the back of the silk blouse and began delicately grazing the warm flesh. He applied a little pressure to the tense muscles and asked in his best witty manner, "You're not gonna shoot me if I straddle your legs, are you?"

"Unfortunately I left my firearm at home so I think you're safe."

It took a mere few seconds to plop his other knee at her hip, effectively imprisoning her between his thighs.
His hands eagerly dove in for the full helping of Savannah's soft, warm skin. As he rubbed at the tension in her lower back, he noticed the image of her tiger tattoo gradually revealing itself. Nonchalantly as possible, he rubbed this way and that, trying to urge the silk bottoms to surrender their secret. Then she did something he wished she hadn't. She pulled the top down and the pants up again.

Frowning, he returned to his work, hearing her groan with obvious delight. He tried again, rubbing until the top rode up slightly. This time she tried turning over, "Ennis, don't, okay?"

He held steady, not allowing her up, "What's wrong?"

"I know you want to see the tattoo but I..." she hesitated, searching for the right words. "I'm self-conscious about it."

"Why?" was all he asked, his fingers working lightly at her lower back, careful now not to reveal the tattoo.

"I got it for a reason, not because I wanted to. It's hiding scars."

His hands instantly halted their movement, "Scars from what?" He'd overstepped and knew it by the way she tensed. He backpedaled, "I understand if you don't want to say. But I've been anxious to see that thing since Georgia told me about it. I promise not to say anything until you're ready to tell me what happened."

She sighed. A few moments passed when he sensed her debating with herself. To help her along, he began working with the large muscles of her back. The fingertips pressed slightly harder then drew down along her spine. The result was a deep, sensual groan from her lips, "Okay," she conceded. "But no questions."

"No questions." He agreed to the condition prematurely for when he lifted the back of the top and lowered the waist of the bottoms, Ennis's temper boiled. All manner of questions flooded his brain. The rage incited his tongue to begin wagging everything from "who" to "how" and "where do I find this person". He pursed his lips hard, trapping the words inside, while his trembling fingers traced the numerous scars. They were long and thin across her back and down past the waist of her panties. He'd wanted to see the tiger but that intent faded as sympathy pains shot down his spine. Someone went to town on this woman's backside with something that had a bite to it.

He turned his attention to the tiger – after all, that was part of why he worked so diligently at the backrub. The tattoo spanned about six inches across the base of her spine and only showed the face of the snarling beast, its thick white teeth ready to bite any unwelcome touch.

Ennis found himself tracing the stripes to the green eyes, from the eyes to the teeth. Most of the tiger's stripes aligned very well with the scars on her back, he noticed. Whoever did the work was a magician. But the tattoo artist couldn't camouflage all the scars. There were plenty still visible.

Ennis glanced up, noting that she'd turned away. That was the last thing he wanted her to do. He wanted her to trust him with anything, everything. He wanted her to share her pain with him, to let him in her life, and to know he loved her with or without the scars.

"Ugly, aren't they?" she said, her voice hushed.

Ennis caught the hint of tears in her voice. He repositioned himself so he could lean down and press a kiss to the nose of the tiger. Instead of tears, he heard her gasp with surprise. *That's better*, he thought. He placed another delicate kiss to the cat's left ear then the right one, and Ennis delighted in the vibration of her shiver. "I think you're beautiful from head to toe," he whispered and kissed the cat's chin – which took him dangerously close to the cleft of her bottom. Savannah's tremulous breath made him harder than stone. "*Ennis*," she pleaded, her voice definitely not teary anymore. It wasn't entirely immersed in heated passion either but it slowly got there. "I know how they look. Don't be so polite," she finished.

"Is that what I'm being?" He didn't quite think so. He also sensed she was fighting off exactly his intention so he upped the ante. His fingertips slipped beneath her top, his hands began caressing her smooth, bare skin. That and her delicate scent brought him dangerously close to losing control of the situation South of the border.

His feather touch provoked a long groan, especially as his hands softly curled around her ribs while his thumbs pressed firmly into the muscles of her back.

Ennis decided hardball was the way to play with Savannah Prince. Bean her upside the head with his feelings – but only to a point – and see what happened.

The scars didn't diminish her inner or outer beauty and they didn't detract from her as a person. Common sense told him why she felt self-conscious. Those were some damn mean looking memories. But, he wanted to say, he was so foolishly in love, he'd probably drown in his desire even if she sprouted another head and two more arms.

He bent down, caged her hips with his hands and planted a hot kiss right below the tiger's chin. He lingered there, even when she jerked with surprise. When she tried to move, it was half-hearted and Ennis kissed each dimple of her buttocks.

Savannah's groan was priceless, "Ennis, please. You're driving me nuts with this. My willpower only stretches so far."

"You said I could see your tiger," he reminded.

"I said you could see it, not seduce it. I'm..." she waited to phrase it appropriately. Finally she gave up, "You're getting me excited, okay? Besides, I agreed to let you see it while under duress."

Ennis's grin broadened to the point it hurt. Her voice quavered throughout the entire rant. He was breaking her, slowly but surely. She thought *this* was duress? He'd barely touched her. Maybe she did care more for him than he thought. The idea alone inspired him to dip down and plant kisses on each of the tiger's ears then one squarely on his nose.

Savannah officially capitulated by sighing and letting her head flop to the pillow, "You're so unfair. Damn tempting and yet so unfair."

Ennis cupped his hands around her waist, allowing himself to measure by feel. Some day he'd hold her as she rode him to her very depth. He'd cherish the day Savannah came to him willingly, wanting him the way he wanted her.

His fingertips curled around to just the right spots while his thumbs held her captive across her back. She fit just right in his hands, no matter where he touched her. He'd "tempted" her enough for one night – now to show her what he could provide in another capacity.

Pressing his thumbs softly into her flesh, he kneaded the tension along her spine. Even she as moaned, he continued with his work. He spent countless minutes roaming her body, memorizing it visually and by touch. His senses took a beating in the process however. Between her sweet sounds, smooth skin, and the delicate scent of flowers, he'd be surprised if sleep *ever* returned to him.

6

The sunshine peeking through the robin's egg blue curtains woke Savannah the next morning – or so she thought. A tapping noise focused her hearing to the door. Either a confused wayward woodpecker landed on the wrong object, or someone was knocking very softly on the door.

She slipped from under the covers and immediately caught sight of Ennis curled on the sofa across the way. She smiled, remembering how he'd massaged her back until she'd fallen asleep. He'd given her plenty to dream about during the night. With his actions, he managed to stir a fire in her that she'd purposefully contained for personal reasons. Being hurt again was not in her plans if preventable. Ennis, however, presented a motivating appeal that proved impossible to overlook. The dreams she dreamed that night were more than sexual. They were downright scary with passion. She hesitated to confess an intense love for Ennis but the dreams refused to ignore those feelings. She'd awakened during the night with an ache not only south of her belly but one in her heart.

The knocking continued, bringing her attention from Ennis to the door. Quietly, she wrapped the amethyst silk robe around her and ambled to the door barefoot. She hated answering the door in such flimsy apparel but her heavy bathrobe was still packed away.

As the knocking increased in urgency, she finished tying the robe's belt and glanced in Ennis's direction. She didn't want to wake her partner. He looked too peaceful and after battling his family the day before, he needed a break.

Cracking the door open, she only saw a broad chest staring back. Then, as the man leaned down, Dane's smiling face greeted her, "Good mornin', Peach. Wanna go for a ride?" He swung an enormous saddle into her vision, making her step back from the door. Dane helped himself to the "invitation" to come in, giving Savannah a chance to appraise his attire. For all intents and purposes, he looked exactly like a typical cowboy. Dressed in worn boots and jeans, sandstone colored jacket zipped to the corduroy collar and a black cowboy hat.

He planted a long gaze on her, "My goodness, you do look sweet in that but I'd slip on some shoes if I were you. Don't want you to get sick. These old nights can get mighty cold out here." He craned his neck around her, searching, "Where's Ennis?"

She softly shushed him then spoke quietly, "You know exactly where he is." Dane was looking right at him, after all. In case he needed guidance, however, she pointed at Ennis, "He's on the sofa. He had a long night and no, that's not what I meant."

Dane chuckled low and winked, "You catch on pretty quick, Peach. You're gonna fit right in with us."

That remained to be seen. So far she fit like a square peg in a round hole. Being around the Rutherford brothers tended to be a mine field, she noticed, and she successfully located every booby trap.

Savannah saw his other arm swing from behind and nearly flinched. She relaxed when she felt him plop a Stetson on top of her head, "There ya go. I picked a darker one – goes with your hair."

Certain she looked as ridiculous as she felt with the cowboy hat tilted harshly to one side, she merely smiled and thanked him. Then she pointed to the saddle, "Is that meant for me?"

He hoisted it about waist level and considered her statement, "Well, it's a bit big for you, plus, if Ennis caught me trying to strap this on you, he'd probably kill me." He waited a moment for the words to soak in then nudged her with his elbow, "I've got your horse ready outside, just needs this. You run along and change – dress warm now – and I'll wait for you right here."

As she turned to wake Ennis, Dane gently grasped her elbow, "We'll let little brother sleep a while. It'll do him good. Don't worry, I'll leave a note tellin' him where we are and what we're doin'."

Savannah could only imagine what the note might say. Then second thoughts about leaving Ennis surfaced. He looked so sweet sleeping. He stirred only a little now and then but always seemed to adopt a childlike innocence upon returning to slumber. She hated to walk out on him even if only to ride a horse. She swiveled to Dane while removing the hat, "I'd rather wait for Ennis to join us."

A crafty grin spread on Dane's rugged features, "Now a sweet little Georgia girl like you wouldn't be scared of a big ol' Texas boy like me, would you?" He shrugged, "I mean, you being a police officer and all. But if you feel more secure with my brother hanging on you, we'll wait."

It was a challenge and she knew it. He also baited her which she realized too. But maybe Dane needed to understand she wasn't "available". She had a feeling Ennis wouldn't be thrilled with her but he'd be less thrilled with his brother. Dane sure had charm and used it. What he didn't understand – she'd seen her share of bullshit too.

Her head tilted slightly and she returned his grin with one of her own, "It'll just take a minute. Wait there," she pointed to a nearby wicker rocker, "and I'll be back."

Dane tipped his own Stetson and winked, "Yes, ma'am."

They stood in a vast expanse of open pasture, their horses patiently awaiting their riders. She'd dressed for the chilly morning as best she could with her jeans, a lightweight pullover and the suede jacket she'd brought. She'd also worn her Nikes, something Ennis promised to change during her stay. He'd promised to purchase a pair of genuine cowboy boots for her. Considering their pointed toes and tall heel, she could hardly wait to slip her feet inside them – not.

Savannah noticed up ahead was the main house – no doubt abuzz at the scene transpiring outside the kitchen window. In the pasture next to them roamed the Hereford cows curiously eyeing the action on the opposite side of the fence.

Savannah appraised her horse. He'd chosen a beautiful blue roan Quarter Horse with a friendly personality. She certainly didn't qualify as an expert on horses but as a kid she'd learned to judge one by its eyes and how calm it was when she approached. The blue roan easily let her pet him much to Dane's delight. Ennis's brother clearly thought this was her first encounter with a horse. Well, it was her first with a horse this *tall...* It was, quite probably, the tallest equine on the Rutherford property. Merely reaching for the saddle horn would bring her to tiptoe, something not lost on either the horse or herself. Leave it to Dane to choose this particular horse for her.

"Up ya go," Dane motioned to her mount. Then he offered, "Need a boost?"

Nice try, Dane... "No thanks. I can manage." In one hand, Savannah took hold of the saddle horn and the horse's mane. Grandpa Prince taught her to hold the latter. In case the saddle wasn't cinched tight enough, she didn't just fall on her ass and possibly get stomped. Her other hand grabbed the back of the saddle and she slid her left foot in the stirrup. Dane stood behind her, "Sure you don't need a boost, Peach? I don't mind."

She heard the smile in his voice. He was staring at her ass, obviously, and at least halfway enjoying it. To cure that problem, she hoisted herself up and to back him off made sure to sweep her right leg out a bit before swinging it over the saddle, "Nope, I got it. Thanks."

She watched Dane study her as she settled comfortably on the saddle. Savannah hoped he soon realized riding a horse *wasn't* as foreign to her as he first thought. Smoothly tugging the reigns to the side she brought the horse effortlessly around to face Ennis's brother, "How do I look up here?"

"Like you're a natural," he approached his buckskin colored horse and swung up in the saddle with much the same ease she had. "Been on a horse before?"

She urged her horse into a gentle gait, circling Dane a couple of times, "Once or twice. Guess it's like riding a bicycle."

Watching in disbelief, Dane visually followed her, "Guess so." To break the routine, he brought his horse alongside hers and reached across, tilting her hat back, "There. I like you better like that."

Really... Savannah readjusted the brim down again somewhat, "Keeps the sun out this way though."

Dane laughed easily, "I'll bet you drive Ennis screwy. He's not used to independent women. Likes his more..." his voice trailed while he searched for the right word.

"Quiet?" she offered.

"Reliant on his strength. It figures he fell for a spunky dame."

She slowed her ride to a near crawl, "What's with this 'dame' stuff, anyway?"

Ennis's brother pretended to cower, "No offense, honest. It's just a term of endearment placed on ladies who come from bluebloods. Ennis said your family was some kind of legend in Georgia."

"*Augusta* is not the state of Georgia. Our grandparents owned orchards and did okay for themselves. We're not the Rockefellers of the South." She realized she sounded vaguely upset but since joining the Atlanta Police, she'd fielded barbs about her family's money and supposed influence. Truth was, with R.J.'s drinking, he made their lives harder, not easier, and the only influence was of the less than helpful variety.

Dane rode fluently, his voice stayed composed, "Savannah, darlin', our family isn't poor either so don't take offense to comments about wealth." He steered his horse to the front to stop her, "I brought you out here to give you a crash course on us. Ennis told us a lot about you but what he made damn sure we understood was his feelings for you. You are his and any one of us brothers who tangles with you will get cracked upside our heads, as was the case yesterday. You'll find a slightly different atmosphere today because Ma had a long talk with us. Not so many remarks to get your hackles up but there'll still be something and Jake'll be the one to say it if it's said. That's just him. He's brash and at times hateful, and he'll never get married unless he finds a woman silly enough to tolerate him."

Jake's personality didn't interest her. She dealt with a variety of personalities on the job, plenty worse than a man who'd yet to mentally mature. What caught her interest was her partner's candidness. "What did Ennis say? His feelings, I mean."

He started a canter similar to a trot, forcing her to catch up. Dane answered, "He's in love, plain and simple."

Savannah drew the reigns up short, causing the horse to voice its displeasure but he stopped anyway.

Dane managed to render her speechless temporarily. Dumbfounded, she stared at the ground, trying to make heads or tails of Dane's statement. She felt nauseous at the concept of marriage. She equated it to a navel piercing – it wasn't for everyone.

Dane ducked down, trying to judge her expression. He guided his mount closer and tipped her hat back, "You okay, honey?"

"Um," she began absently then met his vision, "yeah. Did he *say* he was in love with me?" Savannah noticed Dane's dark eyes focused on her hands. They'd planted themselves on the saddle horn with a death grip, the reigns still securely laced through her thumb and forefinger. She forced herself to loosen the grasp and allow the horse some breathing room. She only wished *she* had some.

"Well," Dane thought back while keeping a close eye on her, "as I recall, he never came out with the words 'I'm in love with Savannah.' His actions speak louder than words. Anyone with two brain cells to rub together can see he's head over heels for you. Jake says he's stupid in love." Dane nodded, "I tend to agree."

But he never said the words. Now she gladly sucked in a long breath. It sounded foolish, she knew, but thinking of marriage – which is the next logical step with love – stopped her cold every time. Love didn't scare her like marriage and Ennis repeatedly joked they would eventually get hitched. Fact was, she possessed strong feelings for him but marriage was a no-no. The knowledge he felt deeply for her warmed her all over. No, it sent her spiraling toward a dangerous inferno she vowed to avoid. Falling for a partner asked for trouble. Acting on those impulses begged for it. Somehow it didn't seem so taboo with Ennis. She felt like she'd known him all her life, not one year. He felt like a partner in life, not just the job. And that's why she questioned her smarts about coming to Texas. Inside, she shrugged. This was a vacation, for God's sake, and she was picking it apart like she did a suspect. Maybe she needed to get away more than she thought. Taking a breath, she finally smiled. Today, though, she'd relax and delight in the information. "How are these horses at racing?" she asked.

Dane caught the dare in her voice, "Fairly good but novice riders shouldn't attempt to try."

"That sounded like a challenge, Dane Rutherford, and I like a good challenge." She further loosened her grip on the reigns and spurred the quarter horse into a full gallop. Savannah held one hand to her hat while the other gave the horse total freedom on the lead. Shortly, Dane's horse pulled up nearly alongside her with him calling for her, "You little stinker. You've been riding horses all your life, haven't you?"

She laughed, "Since I was a kid. My grandfather had horses too. While my brother and sister were picking peaches, I'd be riding. Oh, and Dane? Right now, you're losing." She spurred the horse and smiled as her companion faded further in the distance behind her.

7

"Saw you two out riding this morning," Ennis mentioned at the breakfast table. He split open a biscuit and buttered it with great vigor. Too much vigor, in fact. The light, fluffy biscuit threatened to crumble from the pressure. Savannah came to realize what Ennis meant by being "spitting mad". He looked ready to breathe fire and she prayed the firestorm might subside with a big, hearty meal and an apology. She glanced at Dane who screwed his mouth to the side. He caught the jealousy in his brother's tone too, "She rides pretty good for a little Georgia girl."

Cal spooned a ladle of gravy over his own breakfast, "Last I saw, you trailed in that race. She rides like a damn barrel racer."

"Cal," Bobbi scolded, "don't cuss." She motioned to Monty who decided to pipe up, "You was eating her dust, Dane!"

"*Were* eating her dust," his mother politely corrected to her son's irritation. The annoyance lasted only briefly as Dane mussed his hair. The uncle teased, "Thanks for reminding me, shrimp." Then he turned to a more serious topic – addressing why he and Savannah were together without him, "Ennis, we were just talking. Can't expect me to ignore her. Ma raised us better than that."

Ennis went about his business of buttering another biscuit, "She raised us to respect each other's girls too. I don't go pawing on Bobbi –"

"'Cause I'd kill ya," Cal finished.

Ennis's accusation floored both her and Dane, the latter looking dangerously close to swallowing his tongue, "I wasn't pawing on Savannah, for Pete's sake." He turned sharply to her, "Did I paw you?"

"No, he was a gentleman." She tried to end the confrontation once and for all, "Ennis, I'm sorry I didn't wake you to go riding with us. You'd had a long day and I thought you needed your rest."

Although his tone softened, she still detected sincere hurt, "I'm not angry at you, sugar. I just think the note he left could have been less irritating."

"What did it say?" Savannah now gave Dane a curious glance. He cringed and looked away.

Ennis carefully placed his utensils in the plate as though holding them might encourage drastic behavior of a bloodthirsty kind. He then stared directly at the offending brother, "To the best of my recollection it went like this. 'Sorry you're not here but you know what they say about the early bird. I took Savannah out – don't look for us for a while. Sweet dreams, bro.' Personally, I think I'm allowed to be upset after reading that junk." Obviously venting helped because he took the biscuit he'd just buttered and delicately placed it on Savannah's plate. He followed it up by drenching the biscuit with a ladle of gravy. When he glanced up, he saw everyone except his partner staring at him. He blew out a breath, "What?"

"You suffer from dyslexia as well as jealousy?" Dane inquired then expelled a subdued grunt when Bobbi elbowed him.

Restraining a laugh, Jake piped up next, "You're fixing her breakfast for her, doofus. Like she's a kid." The youngest brother cringed as Bobbi whacked his foot with hers while angling a warning glare at him. He repaid her with the same expression.

Ennis frowned, "For your information, I know what she likes to eat and how she likes it. Don't I?" He looked to her for affirmation.

Savannah nodded, quietly adding, "We've been together a year now so we do tend to take note."

Ennis reached for the salt and began tilting it over his eggs and she finished, "Just like I know he shouldn't use so much salt."

Her partner slumped in defeat, sat the shaker down. Cal chased his breakfast with a hearty swallow of milk, "My God, they're even *acting* married."

Evidently feeling as if he gained some ground in the group, Ennis puffed his chest while buttering his own biscuit, "You do get close as partners so, in a way, it is like marriage."

Savannah saw Dane staring at her, probably searching for a reaction. She felt herself blush as she reached for the salt shaker. Ennis joyfully confiscated it, bringing her attention to him. He explained matter-of-factly, "You don't need it either."

Cal, finished with his meal, stood and tossed his napkin in his plate, "This is getting too weird." He bent to kiss his wife, "See you later, babe," then mussed Monty's hair, "catch you later, squirt." He pointed a semi-accusing finger at Ennis, "Paw my wife and your girl won't have to

worry about pickin' bridesmaids. Without a groom, there's no weddin'."
Cal winked at Savannah, "Bye."

She lifted a limp hand and waved. Bobbi shook her head at her,
"Don't let Cal bother you. He's a big ol' teddy bear."

"Yeah," Jake mumbled. "Like Dane is a 'gentleman'."

Bobbi whacked his foot again. This time, Jake snarled at her.
Savannah tried to display a jovial smile but knew it appeared as tense as
she was. Finally, as though fate intervened, she heard the familiar sound
of "A Little Less Conversation".

As her cell phone sang away in her purse, she noticed everyone's
vision landed on her. "Sorry," she blushed. "I'll take it in the living
room." Grateful for the break, she hauled her purse into the quiet room
and answered it, "Prince." *Please let it be Josh telling me to get back to
work. Please...*

"How's everybody in Tejas?" It wasn't her captain's voice but
Georgia's and she sounded akin to an angel. Savannah realized how
much she missed her sister, even though a mere twenty-four hours had
lapsed.

She heard herself sigh while collapsing on the couch, "Wild as
March hares," she muttered. "I'm tellin' you, Georgia, I'm never
complaining about our family again. Well, with the distinct exception of
Aunt Katherine's brood..."

"If you're counting hours until liftoff, your plane doesn't depart
for another week and a half."

"Oh," she replied darkly, "you called to cheer me up. How
sweet."

Georgia laughed, "Sorry, hon. I wanted to see how Ennis's family was. Are they anything like him?"

"Not at all."

"It's that bad?"

Savannah cringed, frustrated that her point wasn't quite hitting the mark, "No, they're fine. Ennis is just more settled and I'm appreciative of the fact."

"He's acting okay then?"

Savannah glanced around the room to ensure she was alone, "Actually, he's not. His family seems to think we're engaged and he's become very, well, affectionate." She expected her sister to express something in the neighborhood of disbelief. Maybe a hesitation or gasp then say something like, "Not *Ennis*." But Georgia only went, "M-hmm," with a calculating nuance.

"What's that supposed to mean?"

Georgia backtracked, "Oh, nothing. I just kinda figured he'd warm up to you once you were away from the job – and Atlanta."

Savannah slowly allowed her temper to light, "Georgia, so help me if you knew this was happening –"

"Cool off, hon. I only know Ennis likes you and if he wanted you to meet his family… It can only mean one thing really."

Savannah rocketed off the couch, her tone firm and boisterous, "Well, it doesn't mean *that*." From the corner of her eye, she saw everyone in the dining room turn toward her. Shortly after, someone plopped onto the couch and she spun to see Monty, his interest roused. "Whatcha doin'?" he asked.

She swallowed and sat down again, sending her temper to bed, "Talking to my sister."

"Why're ya yellin' at her?"

"Because she deserves it," Savannah deadpanned into the phone. She heard Georgia laugh again, "I'll let you go, hon. Sounds like you're busy."

"You have no idea. Talk with you later." She clicked off her phone and turned her attention to Monty, teasing, "Are you finished eating, young man?"

He shook his head with a sly grin and pointed at her, "But neither are you."

"Yeah, young lady," Ennis suddenly appeared at the door. "How about joining me at least part of the morning?"

He still sounded hurt, Savannah noticed, but he was recovering very well. When he extended his hand to her, she happily wrapped hers around it, "We'll eat breakfast then we'll spend the day together."

Ennis's brow rose in surprise and he looked at his nephew, "What'd you say to her? I like it whatever it was."

Savannah again found herself wearing the cowboy hat and straddling a horse that afternoon. The family had dispersed, some working on the ranch and others hanging around the back porch. Ennis and his partner excused themselves to their own little world of equines and easy conversation.

He waited until they meandered out of everyone's hearing range,

"My family's driving you nuts, aren't they?"

The impromptu question brought her up short. She couldn't be completely honest since her family drove him equally as batty. Ennis sort of chuckled, "It's okay. They drive me crazy too. That's part of the reason I got upset when I realized Dane had you out riding this morning."

Savannah followed his lead with her horse. They made a gentle turn and headed back toward the house, their mounts ambling at a gentle gait. "Oh, and here I thought it was jealousy," she joked.

Ennis slanted her a mischievous grin, "I was oozing jealousy, sugar. Surprised you didn't slip on it when you skedaddled to answer Georgia's call."

"I didn't skedaddle. I..." she paused, searching for the right word.

"Blazed a trail to the living room, far as I could tell. Don't let everyone rattle you. They're screwy but harmless. Well, except Dane."

Savannah glanced toward the house. Bobbi and Mama Rutherford relaxed on the porch, rocking leisurely in cushioned wicker rockers, enjoying the warm breeze. They spent their time drinking coffee and chatting, all while their vision remained riveted on the couple atop the stallions. Occasionally, Savannah saw them lean to the other and say something. The receiving woman always nodded. Savannah directed her attention to Ennis, "I think the closeness is freaking me out. Our family used to be close when I was a kid. Georgia and I were always close to Mama. Daddy was iffy because of his drinking. When Seth left home, everything basically fell apart. Then Georgia moved to Atlanta and the moment I could, I left home. When Mama died, the world collapsed. That's when me and Georgia stuck like glue to each other. Then she got married so, you know..." her voice trailed off.

Ennis reached across and gentled both their horses to a stop. Removing his hat then hers, he then leaned closer, and softly kissed her.

Savannah leaned into the kiss, delighting in his cool fingers cupping the back of her head. His warm lips caressed hers with a passion she doubted she'd ever experienced in her life. Ennis's lips parted at the same time his hand slipped to cradle her hip, drawing her closer. Despite the promise she made to herself before arriving in Texas, she tilted into the kiss and let herself enjoy it. Even if nothing came of it, at least she could remember the kisses she and Ennis shared during their time together here.

Several moments passed when he parted from the kiss, vowing, "You got me, sugar. I'm not going anywhere."

Gazing into his eyes, she swore he meant it. Ennis possessed honesty, a quality she'd never seen before in the male gender. The words he spoke to her were real. She'd learned to spot his fibs on the job. She knew his body language when he lied, recognized the nuance of his voice when he did it. With her, he spoke genuinely and she hoped she sounded equally as genuine with him, "I know and that means more to me than you realize. If it weren't for you sometimes think I'd go as nutty as half my family."

"Or mine," he added.

A hearty laugh sprung from her lips, encouraging him to join in. Both noticed the interest on the porch heightened, more covert whispering followed. The two women nodded with smiles curving their lips.

Ennis winked, "We could cause quite a scandal if we chose to."

Through her smile Savannah cut him a sly glance, "We might just do it too."

8

After a point, news of Ennis's homecoming spread like kudzu in summer. It expanded day and night, taking over households until Savannah determined every living human west of the Mississippi realized he was home again. Bobbi finally explained why the sudden burst of interest. The family waited until they thought Savannah felt more at ease to alert the media and surrounding states. Bobbi further clarified that the phone calls weren't just to welcome Ennis home again, they were also to welcome Savannah to the family. When the phone at the Rutherford house began ringing, nothing short of a baseball bat (which she seriously considered) would shut it up. Friends from all around kept calling until Mama Rutherford decided to hold a barbeque for everyone – weather permitting, of course.

The weather permitted, *of course*, Savannah lamented. What also figured was his family's anxiousness to spread the word of Ennis's impending marriage. The day began pleasingly cool and by afternoon, the sun warmed everyone in the Rutherford's vast "back yard". Wind in West Texas, it turned out, was like humidity in Georgia. It was there and never going away so a person just dealt with it. Like Ennis, she went casual but instead of jeans and charcoal sweatshirt like him, she opted for jeans and a purple pullover to wear that day. The two wandered the yard and mingled as the heavenly smell of barbeque lingered over the crowd. She felt his hand rest at the small of her back which definitely calmed her in front of the mass of strangers. Then it happened…

"Ennis!" a woman shrieked. The shrill sound semi-paralyzed anyone nearest her but thankfully Savannah counted herself spared. Judging by the gleam in the eager woman's eyes, this particular encounter wouldn't be pleasant. The woman charged like a black-haired bull at Savannah's partner who stood rooted to the spot, his eyes so wide Savannah feared they'd fall out.

The woman in the powder blue western type blouse and skin tight jeans couldn't be classified as a raving beauty but she was pretty enough to instill a modicum of insecurity in most living, breathing females. The unknown woman basically launched herself at Ennis, forcing Savannah to step back for safety's sake. Usually an expletive seemed suitable for such an occasion however all Savannah uttered was, "I hope you know this woman since she's climbing on you like a bear."

He tried to answer her but the girl planted a solid kiss on him, preventing any verbal communication past grunting as her weight settled in his arms. When she separated, she again graced the now silent crowd with her voice, "Ennis Daniel Rutherford, where *have* you been? I've been pinin' and pinin' for ya. Ma thought I'd waste away to nothin' since I ain't heard from ya."

Fat chance, Savannah wanted to say then thought better of it. The girl wasn't terribly fat, just plump. She carried the weight well without looking padded in certain places, her rump not being one of them.

Savannah realized everyone looked directly at her instead of the circus in front of her. They all probably expected her to blow her top, rip the woman from his arms and promptly initiate a cat fight.

"Savannah, this is Jenny Lee Crawford, my high school girlfriend," Ennis stated then hesitated with a pleading look at his partner. She wasn't sure why he paused in the middle of introductions but soon found out. "Jenny Lee, this is Savannah Prince. Savannah and I are engaged." He'd said it lowly so no one except the two girls heard him. He also mouthed an apology to Savannah who nearly swallowed her tongue at the declaration.

Jenny Lee slid from his arms, her emotions wavering between shock, hurt and disgust. She then set her sights on Savannah who'd managed to break free of her sudden brain paralysis and extend her hand. Jenny stared at it like Savannah offered her a dead rat, "Geez, Ennis, where'd you find her?"

The emphasis on "her" steamed Savannah. Their introductions weren't even cold and Jenny Lee blatantly drew a line, daring Savannah to step over it. Anyone familiar with the youngest Prince knew that was a mistake. Savannah straightened her shoulders, readied herself for battle, "We work together. We're detectives with the Atlanta Police." *Top that, Blackie*, she challenged silently. Savannah never thought of herself as the jealous type but seeing Jenny Lee Crawford stroke Ennis like a pet cat utterly agitated her. Visions of yanking hair out by the roots floated sadistically in her mind. That, topped with taking a lasso and dragging her raven haired competitor behind a horse all the way to the outskirts of Dallas.

Jenny Lee placed her hand above one ample breast, declaring, "Oh my, a police detective. Isn't that a man's job?"

Both family and friends glue their vision to the conversation. Savannah shrugged at the woman, "I've known some men that weren't capable of tying their own shoes, much less tracking down a murderer. Ennis is one of the smartest cops I know and between the two of us, we make an excellent team." She wasn't about to let some arrogant little snit get the drop on her. What Jenny Lee didn't realize was Savannah and Ennis were respectably secure enough *not* to get too riled upon an interloper's arrival but watching the woman now, Savannah felt her confidence slipping…

The way Jenny Lee flipped her long black hair while talking to Ennis mined the depths of her temper. Jenny lit the fuse to the dynamite when she began touching him on the arm, stroking his cheek and basically climbing into his arms.

Savannah considered herself protective of her partner, just as he was of her, but the protective nature resided in her gut. When she sensed him in danger, a stirring occurred in her stomach that verged on a twinge. The current sensation dwelled in her heart and damn if it didn't hurt. It twisted in her chest when Ennis laughed with Jenny Lee, and it sank to her toes if he simply brushed his ex on the arm. Savannah remembered the soft touch, the way he drew his fingers down her arm, down her back. Ennis didn't "touch" a woman, he caressed her. Witnessing another woman's reaction to his touch drove her temper into the red zone.

Savannah looped her arm through Ennis's, claiming him once and for all, "He's definitely the best *I've* ever had."

The comment splattered on Jenny Lee like scalding oil. She gasped quietly then slinked off by herself. Savannah hoped she might leave altogether once she drew her own line in the dirt. The female cop didn't dare Jenny to step across, she vividly described through visual contact what would happen if she did. Savannah soon discovered Jenny Lee Crawford either possessed no common sense or held no regard for her own life.

After searching the grounds for Ennis, she spotted him behind a barn located several yards ahead, the victim of an abduction. Jenny Lee barricaded him with both hands – when one wasn't trying to unbutton his shirt. Savannah's anger rose while Ennis captured Jenny's hand and removed it with a friendly albeit stern warning. The woman's hand returned like a bee to a flower. Savannah heard him sigh while again plucking her greedy grasp off his shirt.

"Hey, Peach," a voice said a little too close to her ear.

She jumped and glanced over her shoulder at Dane, greeted him. She tried to sound congenial. After all, Dane didn't act too fond of Ms. Crawford either. He lifted a lasso to her vision, "How 'bout I show you the fine art of roping? You're a natural, I can tell. If you can aim a gun, you can aim a rope."

She declined but promised a rain check. Dane patted her back, "If you're sure. Remember, anytime you want that lesson, I'm here."

Savannah thanked him but for now she needed to police Jenny

Lee and her wayward hands and lips. She surveyed the enormous yard until spying Jenny with Ennis again, her mouth going a hundred miles an hour. The woman was still on the make, even though Ennis told her he was spoken for. That pissed Savannah off beyond words. Jenny Lee had no comprehension of "engaged" except with her mouth. She engaged it quite well and quite often, Savannah noticed.

"Something still got you bent out of shape, Peach?" Dane, at some point, had sidled up behind her again. He followed her line of vision, "M-hmm, I was wonderin' how long it'd take." Dane stepped in front of Savannah, enjoying her antics to angle a view of Ennis and his ex, "If brains were leather, she couldn't saddle a flea but don't underestimate Jenny Lee Crawford, my dear. She's out for Ennis like a dog in heat."

Savannah remained quiet and brooding. She fantasized about all manner of tortures for a chesty black-haired gatecrasher. The woman simply had to be dealt with and soon.

Dane bent down so their vision locked, "You want that lasso lesson yet?"

No, she wanted to annihilate the presumptuous female using Ennis as a step ladder. She wanted to chase her off and make her run like her feet were on fire and her ass was catchin'. Why Dane offered the lasso lesson *right then* escaped her. Until… She felt her brow dip lower as the indisputable urge of wicked behavior overtook her, "Now that you mention it, yes, I do."

"Just so happens I have a rope right here," he waved everyone back to make room. He stepped behind her, instructed her how to hold the rope, widen the loop, windup and pitch. She took a couple of practice throws at an empty beer bottle then a tree stump. She missed the bottle but nailed the stump.

Savannah glanced up to see Ennis watching while talking absently to his high school girlfriend. His expression conveyed a high degree of exhaustion and indeed, he attempted unsuccessfully to extricate himself from her company. The problem resided in Jenny Lee's ability to speed talk. Savannah wasn't entirely sure how many words per minute the girl spoke but she'd put any native Yankee to shame.

Ennis lifted his shoulder in a subdued shrug to Savannah who fully intended to rescue him, albeit in an unconventional way. With lasso in hand, she widened the loop and as if by telepathy, Dane waved the gawking crowd closer, delight showing in his voice, "Hey y'all, watch this."

Savannah slanted him a mischievous smile, "Back home those particular words send people running for cover."

"Yeah, try growing up with three brothers. Right now, I think Jenny Lee oughta be diving for cover herself."

Savannah started her windup with the lasso, "No, but she best back away or you'll be teaching me how to hog-tie too."

By now a mass of people, including Ennis's family, gathered to watch. Ennis kept on being bored out of his skull and Jenny Lee floored the accelerator with her rate of speech. She capped her current rambling off with a boisterous laugh that Ennis flinched at but forced a laugh as well.

When the lasso gained enough momentum, Savannah lifted the

spinning rope above her head, her aim – straight at her partner. The instant she released it, she knew she hit her mark. The lasso slipped effortlessly around Ennis's shoulders and dropped to his elbows when she pulled back, cinching the loop around him. Appalled, Jenny Lee let a burst of a scream that sent everyone into a fit of laughter. Savannah merely grinned as she reeled in her partner, hand over hand, with the rope. That stunt alone seemed to cool Jenny Lee's enthusiasm considerably. When Ennis embraced his partner with a buoyant laugh, she could see Jenny Lee deflate even further. It served her right, Savannah thought.

After the escapade, the party atmosphere put her at ease until someone, usually a woman, broached the subject of Savannah and Ennis's relationship. Savannah deferred to her partner to answer all inquiries. In retrospect, not the brightest decision she'd made considering all the knowing looks thrown her way. Knowing Ennis, he used terminology that didn't confirm nor deny an impending marriage but by various expressions, she recognized which road the guest's minds took.

Later that afternoon, she overheard references to a cold front due in that night complete with snow, and indeed, the sky darkened before evening and her knee began aching. Normally that was her gauge for bad weather. Forget weathermen, she heeded the warning her knee gave and by evening it hurt enough she took a prescription painkiller for it.

Strangely, during the party, she detected no concern in the partygoers or Ennis's family regarding the weather. No one thought it warranted even five minutes conversation, especially when she mentioned the indigo hue of the approaching clouds. Dane drew her against him

with one arm and squeezed her shoulders accordion-like, "Don't worry
'bout it, Peach.   A little snow never hurt anyone."   He turned his
attention to their listeners, "She's a sweet girl but frets entirely too
much." They all indulged in a hearty laugh except Savannah who rubbed
at her knee and wandered back to Ennis to ask his opinion about the
ominous horizon.

He cupped her chin in his hand, and his gentling touch helped.
What truly calmed her was the brief peck on the lips he gave her,
"What're you worried about, sugar? Being snowed in together isn't such
a bad thought.   Many productive hours can be spent in our majestic
ranch house."

She smiled, softly nudging him with her elbow, "What's ailin'
you, Rutherford? You've been goofy ever since I got here."

He shrugged, allowing his silence to speak for itself.

She nudged him again, "I wouldn't mind spending time alone
with you. I just don't like the image of snow to the rooftops."

Ennis brought her up close, "I love a woman with an active
imagination. Sugar, we rarely have storms that bad. It may get knee
deep now and again, but it doesn't prevent us from motivating where we
need to be."

9

Despite Ennis's positive outlook the day before, the dawn's early light revealed the fact Mother Nature busied herself overnight with a furious potency. Savannah drew the curtain back from the window and beheld a sight every kid loves – and every adult dreads. A blizzard. The bitter wind howled, shooting snowflakes like missiles. She doubted the possibility of motivating in an actual vehicle with wheels. More likely a horse – a spirited one – would be the mode of travel that day. A smooth white blanket covered the pasture outside, belying the true danger of the storm. What looked like three inches of snow, in actuality, added up to at least eight as evidenced by the fencepost she employed as a visual ruler. Eight inches of dazzling white trouble with plenty more on the way according to the clouds.

Savannah heard a stirring behind her and soon after, felt Ennis's warmth press against her back. He swept her hair aside and planted a tender kiss at her nape, "You're up early."

"Wind woke me up," she answered, not bothering to hide the fact their ranch house stood in the middle of Old Man Winter's playground.

Ennis wrapped his arms around her, bringing her closer then

focused his vision outside. Initially, he appeared as stunned as she had, "What the hell... No one said anything about this much snow. Dane and Jake keep track of the weather like owls tracking mice."

"Maybe the owls had too much barbeque and beer yesterday. Dulled their abilities to predict blizzards." Savannah hated to think they purposely kept mum about the upcoming weather but truth was they made sure the animals had plenty of food and were sheltered properly. She also noticed Dane paid particular attention to their own needs. He'd stocked the main house and their little ranch house with food, extra blankets and two Arctic Drifter coats, the latter hanging like omens across the room from her. She noticed them when they retired from the party the night before. Evidently Dane had been busy preparing for a storm he didn't see coming.

Clearly Ennis also questioned his brother's motives because his vision settled on the heavy duty ranch coats. Savannah's travel plans just disappeared on the wind like all the tiny snowflakes zipping past the window, "Well, I'd better call Georgia and let her know what's happened. Then we both get to answer to the boss about taking more time off." She stepped from Ennis's hold to retrieve her purse. Ennis stopped her, "Let's not get ahead of ourselves. The airport is probably still open and–"

"Ennis, I'm not leaving here in this kind of weather, no matter if the airport's open or not. I don't like flying anyway but flying in snow and worrying about iced up wings will only serve to disconnect any sanity I have left. I'm rescheduling the flight." She took her cell phone, punched it on then just as quickly she closed it and placed it back in her purse with a resigned sigh.

Ennis uneasily inquired, "Change your mind?"

Savannah angled toward the coffee pot, her fingers threading her hair, "The storm knocked out the cell service. I'll have to call from here or your mother's." She poured coffee into the empty mug for Ennis and refilled hers, wondering how she'd explain this to her sister. Savannah faithfully called every day but Georgia hadn't sounded right the day before. Her sister's mood wilted considerably and Savannah failed to coax the cause from her.

A light touch at her waist brought her thoughts racing to the here and now. Ennis's fingers slipped beneath her top making her totally aware of where his warm flesh touched hers. His hand splayed out across her belly, the heat from his palm made her stomach flutter. He drew her close until she stood flush against him, "It's just snow, sweetheart. Plus, it gives us more time together," his hot breath caressed her ear. "That's not so bad, right?"

She wanted to curse the snow and unexpected circumstances but his fingertips softly stroked her flesh and scattered all reason. Ennis had always been a temptation for her and she'd fought every womanly desire not to indulge. Every time he touched her, the yearning returned full force, every time he kissed her, she nearly lost control. All he wanted now was agreement about the storm so she answered, "Right." Savannah felt the blood race in her veins, her cheeks blushed crimson. Her voice had sounded low and rough and would bet her life Ennis detected it too.

Sure enough, there was a smile in his words, "Why, there's no telling what we might decide to do." He punctuated his statement with a slow, heated kiss beneath her ear then one to her shoulder.

Savannah turned in his arms, the thread of willpower fraying at an alarming rate. She cupped his face in her hands and Ennis leaned toward her, both realizing what the other craved. Her lips brushed his and both released a long breath as if the kiss finally broke the tension. Ennis cupped the back of her head to deepen the kiss when a raucous noise filled the room…

The phone rang almost on cue. Noticeably disappointed at the interruption, Savannah eased away from the steamy kiss, leaving him as frustrated as she. He wheeled, vowing a number of indecipherable cruelties toward the caller.

He felt it in his heart. He'd practically defeated Savannah's stubborn streak when some damn idiot barged in electronically. That, along with the thought Dane deliberately misled his partner, boosted his temper a notch. It was a beautiful fantasy having her stuck there in a blizzard. No romance novel could have designed it better. But Dane fancied himself the hero of the story, not Ennis. He wanted Savannah to stay in Texas with *him*, a rancher's wife no doubt, raising a rabble of kids named Dane Jr. or Dane the Second. No, Ennis would not stand for such an outrage. If the person on the phone happened to be his brother, he was about to find out how close Ennis was to strangling him.

Ennis jerked the phone from its cradle, "Yeah?"

"Is that any way to greet your mother?" the voice on the other end inquired.

The sound of his mother's voice served only to release an infinitesimal amount of rage boiling inside him, "Sorry, Ma. What's up?"

"Breakfast is cooking and you and Savannah need to get on down here. Might have to stay here tonight if the snow doesn't let up."

Don't think so... Hell, he could still feel Savannah's full, plump breasts against his chest, he still tasted her on his lips. Worst of all, he sensed her desire burning as fierce as his. She finally *wanted* him... Deciding to ignore his mother's last comment, Ennis rubbed his forehead in frustration, "Did Dane and Jake get the horses put up?"

After a short hesitation his mother replied, "Yes, why?"

"And the cows. Did they get them squared away last night?"

"M-hmm. Why're you asking about the livestock?"

Right about then the light bulb blinked on in his brain, "Dane tell you this storm was coming and how bad it might get?"

"He said there was snow headed our way and it looked like it'd hang around a day or two. Ennis, what's got you so riled?"

Now he was so mad he could hardly speak. His brother trapped Savannah here with full knowledge of her scheduled flight back to Atlanta. Trapped so he could make moves on her, undoubtedly. "Savannah's flight was tomorrow. She promised her family she'd be back–" his tongue immediately seized up once he caught sight of Savannah's incredulity. He mentally tiptoed backward until making connection with his voice, "She doesn't mind staying a little longer but Dane should have told her."

His mother adopted a knowing tone, "Ennis, honey, stop

worrying about your brother. He's not trying to ruin your life or take your sweetheart –"

"But you'd better keep an eye on him, Ennis," Bobbi piped up in the background.

"See?" Ennis said, grateful his sister-in-law validated his concern. "Even Bobbi says I oughta hog-tie that bastard and leave him for dead." He saw Savannah's mouth gape and shook his head, mouthing "not really". Ennis changed the subject, "We'll be down shortly. Did my industrious brother leave us means for travel?"

"Said he left you a truck but, honey, the snow might be too deep for it. He said there are two horses in the stable across the way."

"Well, at least he didn't want us to freeze to death before I could kill him."

Savannah could have sworn she'd stepped into the frontier. Snow as far as the eye could see – with the distinct exception of the ranch house and main house and a few smaller buildings she could barely recognize as stables. The snow whipped fiercely around her but thanks to Ennis, only her eyes noticed. He'd dressed her better than a concerned mother swaddling her infant before daring outside with her. She was lucky her arms and hands moved for all the layers of clothing he'd wrapped her in. She produced a fairly convincing argument only to be tenderly shushed by her partner. She finally resigned herself to the fact Ennis tried to protect her. *While in Texas, do as the Texans,* she relented.

Savannah now rode alongside her partner, thoroughly shrouded beginning with her hat which he'd socked down on her tighter than the cap on a bottle of Budweiser. Beneath that was a wool scarf he scrounged from the chest of drawers in the house. He'd draped it around her face and neck until she felt positively claustrophobic underneath it. Still lower, her mauve sweatshirt cloaked with the Artic Drifter – "warmer than goose down" as Ennis said – cinched down in every way possible and the collar flipped up around her neck. Engulfing her hands were thick well-worn gloves. She wore her jeans but "to cut the wind and snow" Ennis outfitted her with a pair of genuine leather chaps and her Justin cowboy boots bought specially for her by Ennis just days earlier.

The boots became an awkward challenge to undertake, being from the loafer and sneaker breed she was. First time out, she adapted an ungainly, embarrassing gait that teetered her side to side when she shifted one foot in front of the other. She was quite certain the image was reminiscent of her toddler days when she first ventured from knees to feet for walking.

Savannah embarked on the mission only in Ennis's company since she hadn't felt in the right mood to be laughed at. How people actually walked in cowboy boots puzzled her. In the process of her bewilderment, Savannah finally decided that being bowlegged was paramount to motivating in such unwieldy footwear. Ennis, bless his heart, restrained the urge to laugh.

By evening's end, thankfully, walking became slightly smoother but still painful. When she pulled them off, the beginnings of blisters graced her weary vision. *What women do for men*, she'd thought grimly and with a fine thread of humor. Ennis insisted she take home a pair of true cowboy boots and further insisted he buy them. In turn, she felt equally obliged to wear them. Cowboy boots were the scourge of humankind, she bemoaned. A plague heaped upon the white rancher by the Mexican, a revenge of sorts and it worked like a charm. When Ennis caught sight of her blisters and pained expression, he massaged her feet with the tenderness of a lover. Ennis's foot rubs, she'd finally decided, were well worth the pain and effort.

They approached the main house where they dismounted and led their horses to shelter. The snow accumulated too deep along the back door so they stepped inside the back door to stomp the snow off their boots. Savannah's stomach growled at the aroma of fresh baked biscuits and frying bacon. When she rounded the corner to the kitchen, she expected Mama Rutherford would be scrambling a passel of eggs for the bevy of hungry mouths. Before coming to Texas, Savannah never saw such an enormous bowl of scrambled eggs in her life. In her family, it would have served everyone plus ten more. In Ennis's, the bowl sat empty before second servings were even thought of.

Today, she'd grab a spoonful of eggs, and at least two of Bobbi's giant biscuits complete with the most delicious gravy ever gracing her tongue. One thing about the Rutherford women – they could out-cook anyone in quality *and* quantity. In Mama, Savannah finally found someone to rival Georgia's cooking. She dreaded going home because she'd no doubt gain a significant amount of weight during her trip and she feared Georgia would fail to recognize her at the airport. Even so, Savannah desperately looked forward to the feast – the only trick was unwrapping herself so she could eat.

The instant she and Ennis stepped inside the house, all eyes riveted on her. Dane, with a most amused expression, drew nearer and said, "I'm assuming Savannah's in there somewhere."

Mama Rutherford and Bobbi swiveled from the stove to view a sight that widened their eyes in a way that Savannah thought they'd seen the Abominable Snowman.

"Good Heavens, what happened?" Mama asked.

"Gracious, Ennis, is she able to walk?" was Bobbi's generous contribution.

Ennis puffed up like the proverbial toad, "She's not used to this kind of weather. Didn't want her catching cold."

Bobbi rushed to Savannah's aide and began unbundling her from the top down, "Well, she can't even catch her breath right now." Once free of the muffler, Savannah took a rather deep breath but not a loud one – she hated to offend Ennis. He'd spent the better part of twenty minutes trussing her up so, and while trying and exhausting, his efforts were appreciated – even if she was beginning to sweat.

About to answer, Savannah gasped instead when Dane kneeled in front and began fiddling with the buckle to the chaps, a buckle positioned an ample distance below her navel. "Settle down, honey," he said. "You'll feel better once these are off." One tug later he grunted, "Cripes, Ennis. It's not a corset. No wonder she's turnin' blue."

Less than two seconds later Ennis's hands replaced Dane's, "I got 'em on her, I'll get 'em off."

Savannah glanced at Mama Rutherford then Bobbi, her expression wavering between concern and a plea for help. Bobbi spoke for both women, "Rutherford men are *so* helpful. They practically smother a woman with their attentions." She elbowed Dane in the ribs and mumbled, "Step aside, Dane."

Dane shielded himself from additional attacks but backed up a step, allowing Ennis to take over. Savannah, hiding the beginnings of a smile, started unbuttoning the coat, "And I thought Georgia was famous for Southern hospitality."

Dane flashed a rather flirtatious grin, "Everything's bigger in Texas, darlin'. Need some assistance with your coat?" An almost instantaneous groan floated past her. Its source: Bobbi, who looked ready to belt him again. The spunky redhead balled her fist and socked him in the shoulder, "Mind your manners, you galoot."

Savannah felt Ennis's temper work through his touch. He tugged a bit hard trying to release the chaps at her waist. Savannah tried not to react but had to steady herself on Dane's shoulder anyway, "Where's Monty?"

Bobbi returned to her work at the stove, "Oh, he spent the night with a friend. They like to ride horses in the gully when they're together. Though they'd better be inside now. Snow's too deep to be out there."

With another solid tug from Ennis, Savannah frowned. His kneeling in front of her finally got the best of her. With him struggling with the buckle located so close to her crotch, she decided the scene lingered between suggestive and inappropriate. She blushed, put a hand to his shoulder, "I can handle it from here."

"Stay put," was his instruction given much gentler than his current touch.

Savannah glanced over at Dane who winked. Ennis tugged harder, telling her he still fumed over his brother's presumptuous manner. She concluded that asking her partner a question might diffuse his anger, "What's the gully?"

Finally the buckle on the chaps released – much to her delight. Ennis unzipped the left chap.

In the meantime, Dane watched and Savannah broke another sweat from his intense scrutiny. The fact Ennis removed the chaps shouldn't have bothered her. It shouldn't have felt like he slowly undressed her and it damn sure shouldn't have interested Dane so much. Even as his brother's gaze roamed her from head to toe, she sensed he knew every thought racing through her mind – and it drove her positively crazy.

Another hot rush of blood stained her cheeks as Ennis answered, "It's a small canyon down at the back of the ranch. It's a nice place to ride on clear days. Today though, it'd be tough to see where you are."

The mention of it seemed to inspire Bobbi toward the telephone, "Speaking of the weather, I'd best find out if Monty's ready to come home. I don't think that storm's letting up for anything or anyone."

While Bobbi dialed, Ennis seethed. Savannah could tell the innocent statement grated his nerves. Even now he was convinced Dane concealed the information so she'd be trapped in Texas, so to speak. She never realized her partner possessed such a strong jealous streak – especially over her.

"Savannah, honey," Mama Rutherford called.

The calling drew her into the past. She could still hear her mother call her with those very words and before she realized it, she'd responded, "Yes, Mama?" Then, like a curveball, it hit her and nearly knocked her sideways. The room grew quiet as all present turned to her, surprised. It was the first time she'd acknowledged Ennis's mother as her boys and Bobbi did. Until that moment, Mama Rutherford had been addressed as "ma'am". Now her cheeks deepened from the initial shade of crimson to a plum. If a person's head could possibly blast off their shoulders from embarrassment, the Rutherford ceiling was about to gain a new vent.

"Well," the older woman beamed from ear to ear, "it's about time you disposed of the formalities." She wiped her hands on a nearby dishcloth and set her sights on Savannah. The intrinsic desire to flee the kitchen became impossible as not only Mama but Dane wrapped her in a hug that literally stole her breath. Their hold grew so tight she felt almost positive it was a first cousin to hazing. Dane kissed her cheek, "Why, it's just like she's already part of the family. We got our own Georgia Peach to squeeze."

The worst of the embrace had passed Savannah assumed – either that or she'd lost all feeling and couldn't judge anymore. But Mama Rutherford stepped back and began speaking softly, "I always knew Ennis was a man of fine taste and judgment and he obviously looked long and hard for a wife. From the time we've spent together, I know you and I will become much closer. Now, honey, I know your mama's gone and you'll always miss her but I want you to know you're like a daughter to me already." Mama Rutherford proceeded to reestablish the bear hug at an alarming, nearly smothering degree.

Savannah found it terribly difficult to breathe, much less utter a word. For some reason Ennis continued to nurture the illusion of their "engagement" and would clearly perform CPR on it if the idea had the audacity to die down. Knowing her partner, somewhere he stowed paddles and a respirator lest she herself tried to slay the concept of their impending marriage. Why he didn't enlighten his eager family she didn't know. She did *care* but she didn't know why he clammed up or refused to disclose the truth. She liked his family, screwy as they were. For the past several days they'd grown on her more like ivies than mold. They didn't want to let her go and frankly the feeling was becoming mutual.

A hand on her shoulder dragged her from her thoughts. It was Ennis who whispered, "I'm sorry about all this, sugar. This whole trip isn't what I had in mind for you."

Savannah closed her eyes as his warm breath heated her, caressed her cool ear. For the first time since stepping off the plane, the talk of marriage didn't grate on her. Ennis's sincere apology served to deepen her affection for him. In a way he had a point. How could he stop a train wreck? Except it didn't feel like a train wreck now. It felt like – home.

She turned in his embrace and saw his apologetic expression. Smiling, she lifted to her toes and pressed a kiss to his lips. The kiss clearly stunned him since his brow shot straight up, and his lips, initially firm, softened with the continued contact. She lingered until feeling him respond then briefly pulled away, whispering back, "Don't be sorry. I'm not."

The shade of purple he turned practically matched hers. He

ignored the playful nudge Dane gave him and smiled down at her, "I love you."

Her eyes widened in what Ennis interpreted as fear. Her heart interpreted it differently. While her panicked partner scrambled to salvage the moment, she basked in the significance of the words. The three little words most women crave to hear. The same words she cringed to hear – until now. Somehow they just sounded… right.

Meanwhile, Ennis bore the expression of a frightened deer unsure where the nearest hiding place might be. Before being able to calm Ennis about his sudden utterance, she heard him mumble in a near whisper, "Sugar, what I meant –"

"Oh my God," Bobbi cried, tearing the apron away. Spilling tears, she ran past everyone to the entry.

"Bobbi," Mama Rutherford called as she rushed by. Her alarmed behavior told Savannah one thing. Monty was in trouble.

Ennis and Dane stared at each other searching for an answer while Mama ran after Bobbi. The men followed with Savannah close behind. She heard them discussing various reasons for such an outburst and clued them in, "Something's happened to Monty."

The mention of the youngster immediately spurred the men faster.

The trio dashed to the living room until they faced Bobbi. The frantic woman's hands fumbled with the bulky coat until dropping it. Ennis grabbed the coat while Dane caught her by the arms, "What's wrong with Monty?"

Bobbi wrestled to free herself. After a point she surrendered and dissolved in another round of tears, "He's out in this storm. I have to find him."

Ennis joined Dane trying to calm her, "He's been along that road a million times, Bobbi. He'll be home soon but we'll go pick him up for you."

"No, Ennis, you don't understand." Frustrated, she swiped away her tears, "He's been out in the storm since early this morning. He left Rosemary's house at seven. He wanted to get home before the snow was too deep."

Savannah had a few questions about the explanation. Not many people felt safe enough to allow their children to walk home alone, especially for a considerable distance. She wondered about Rosemary's common sense and decency. The storm raged all night – why send a child out alone? Why let him go if he insisted? The dangers drastically outweighed the benefits.

In this situation, she chose to heed her mama's advice. "Don't get involved if it isn't your business to begin with", or sometimes she shortened it to "Leave it be."

Savannah brushed past her partner, heading for the coat she'd managed to shed no more than ten minutes earlier. Ennis sidled up behind her, his arm blockading her access to the coat, "You're staying here. You don't know the terrain or where you are in that storm."

They all watched the female cop bristle, her brow sinking to give her an impressively intimidating glare, "I'm going. I may not know this land as well as you but there's a boy out there needing help." Her expression backed him off a step, allowing her to pluck the heavy coat from the wall hook. "You helped me with Lindsey and I'm helping with Monty."

While Savannah took the hat and muffler in hand, Mama Rutherford approached in a gentle attempt to dissuade her, "Honey, Ennis is right. It would be best for you and Bobbi to stay here while the men go search for Monty."

Ennis shrugged on his coat, finally surrendering to his obstinate partner, "Ma, it's no use. She's determined to go so let's get busy."

Savannah smiled at Ennis's mother and added a tiny shrug, "He knows me better than I think."

Mama voiced her displeasure but in the end settled on shaking her head with a sigh, "I don't like it one bit but if you insist on going, just be careful."

Savannah agreed and plopped the hat on her head and began to wrap the muffler around her face when she stopped. It struck her that something else dire might occur if she left – unless she forewarned Mama Rutherford first, "Georgia will be calling soon and when she can't reach my cell phone, she'll probably call here. Would you mind explaining what's happened and that I'll talk to her later?"

"I sure will, honey. Don't worry about a thing."

"She's a worrywart."

Ennis looped his hand through her arm, tugging her along, "They'll get along famously." He winked at his mother, "Georgia worries like Mama does so they can reassure each other."

As Savannah and Ennis passed by Dane, she heard the older brother mutter, "I've seen mules less obstinate than your woman."

10

Savannah swung into the saddle then shoved the hat down tighter on her head. It was difficult to comprehend a place on earth where the wind blew so incessantly hard. Every snowflake stung like ice on her cheeks, the wind drove the chill to the bone. She shrugged deeper into the Arctic Drifter coat only to hear Dane yell against the howling wind, "Sure you wanna go? This is some mighty treacherous land in this weather."

She tilted into the wind in a futile attempt to cut the bite, "I'm sure. I want to make sure Monty's safe."

Dane's large, gloved hand held his hat to his head as a gust of wind blew past, "They sure grow you Georgia girls tough."

"It's a holdover from the Civil War."

"Let's hit the road then. Cal an' I will take the road and you an' Ennis search along the gully." He retrieved a walkie-talkie from his coat and addressed only Ennis, "We'll check with each other every ten minutes."

The group split up, Cal and Dane heading north toward the road, while she and Ennis proceeded south to the gully. Savannah let her partner take the lead. The last thing in her plans was suddenly running out of road, plunging into a chasm and finding herself staring skyward. While they rode, Ennis informed her of the gully's depth and a tumble that great maimed on a good day, killed on a bad one. He took time to explain the distance separating their ranch from Travis and Rosemary's and the fact walking home was the typical mode of travel for the boys. She refrained from asking the questions plaguing her since Bobbi's phone call. Ennis, though, seemed to read her mind, "It's not like Monty to strike out in a snowstorm and its sure not like Rosemary to let him. Could be neither knew how bad it was."

"Could be," she agreed. "I just hope we find him soon."

Less than ten minutes elapsed when a thread of uncertainty wound through her gut. Was she insane or just stupid? Ennis was right. She had no inkling where they plodded to. Unlike back home, landmarks were scarce. The posts of the barbed wire fence were the only visible markers. The Rutherford acreage ended about fifty feet from the gully, she estimated, and the longer she and Ennis rode, the further away the ranch grew, the houses and barns fading into a white abyss that reminded her of a Louis L'Amour book she once read. On the upside, she had Ennis whereas the protagonist of the L'Amour book had no one with whom to weather the brutality of the storm.

"You havin' second thoughts?" Ennis called from beside her.

Savannah hunkered down in the coat before facing him. In that time she attempted to remove the doubt from her expression to settle for downright misery instead, "I want that boy home with his mother."

Ennis flinched at the snow whipping under his hat and sidled closer to her, "Then you wonder why my family will skin me if I don't marry you? Hell, if I blink Dane will take my place." He must have spied what he considered uneasiness in her features at the mention of marriage since he reached out to touch her arm, "I'm not asking for a commitment. I'm only asking that you keep an open mind and I'm asking you not to elope with my brother."

The last statement cracked a smile, "I can keep an open mind and Dane's too rascally for me so stop worrying." She returned to searching the depths of the gully. If a child came through earlier that morning, she feared the footprints were history considering the depth of snow and lashing winds swirling through. "Should we go down in there to search?"

Ennis shook his head, "Not yet. Let's look from up here then we'll circle back and go down if we have to. The ledges get tricky even in good weather."

Savannah tentatively glanced around her at the white landscape quickly becoming unrecognizable, "Do you have a compass?" She saw him about to laugh then he thought better of it. To her relief, he nodded, "In my pocket. What's the matter, 'fraid I'll get us lost?"

"No, afraid the snow will."

For the next several minutes, they searched visually, calling Monty's name but never seeing evidence of him. Dane's voice rattled from the walkie-talkie prompting Ennis to answer. The handheld hissed and crackled but Savannah caught enough of Dane's statement to realize they had no success on their end.

Ennis toyed with the radio a moment then spoke into it, "Mama, any news there?"

A brief silence ensued then Mama Rutherford's voice appeared,

"Nothing here. Rosemary sent Casey and Travis out from their place. Between the mess of you, someone's gotta find him. How's Savannah holding up?"

Ennis glanced her way and smiled, "Like a rancher's daughter. I'll check back with you soon." He fiddled with the walkie-talkie again – Savannah finally assumed he changed frequencies on it – then pocketed it.

They rode in silence for another twenty minutes. Savannah huddled down in the coat, gathered the collar to her neck. Winter in the Plains was better experienced than read about, she decided. The majority of outsiders probably discounted the descriptions as folly of an inspired writer. Savannah knew better now. The howling wind, horizontal snow that struck bare skin like blowing sand, the bitter cold, she believed it *all*.

She dared to ride closer to the ravine's edge. Ennis saw her veer and swung his mount toward her, yelling against the wailing gusts, "Come back this way. You don't know where the edge is. The snow gives a false sense of security."

Right in the middle of his statement, she caught sight of something and abruptly pulled her horse to a stop. "What color is Monty's coat?"

Ennis disregarded his own advice and sidled his steed near hers, "What do you see?"

"There's something red, bright red, down there," she pointed then pulled the collar together to block the snow. From above it appeared small, perhaps something the storm's wind blew in. Savannah bent down, shielding her eyes with her hand. Heavy snow obscured the view, preventing her from identifying the mystery below. Most of the snow whipped past her but some caught the ledge, swirled down the side and around the red object.

Ennis grabbed the walkie-talkie, "Mama, ask Bobbi what color coat Monty's wearing." He pressed the speaker to his ear to hear the response. Savannah heard a crackle of noise but not the answer. Ennis, too, had problems understanding and covered his other ear with his hand, "Did you say red?" He listened again then, "I think we might have him in the gully. Tell the boys to head out this way." He pocketed the walkie-talkie and nodded, "It's gotta be him."

Savannah dismounted first. Her partner objected, "You're staying right here. Let me and the boys go after him. They'll be here shortly."

Her hands clamped to her hips, "And in the meantime Monty's freezing. I'm going down there, Ennis." She tested the ledge with her boot heel, searching for the rim. Some gully, she lamented. She hated it when Ennis was painfully correct. The abyss she stared into resembled a small canyon. The bottom – if that really was the bottom – looked twenty or thirty feet down. A stern grasp took her arm, turned her to face Ennis's riled features. He left no doubt where he stood on the situation, "You're not going, Savannah. One wrong step and you could kill yourself."

A bitter squall blew past, forcing one hand to her hat to hold it in place, "And the danger is any less for you and your brothers? I'll be careful."

He reached to stop her and she side-stepped – a move that took the footing from under her. Savannah clutched at the ledge only to grab fistfuls of snow. Ennis unsuccessfully fumbled for her hands before she slid out of reach. Savannah heard him calling her name even as her foot caught on something solid, stopping her descent. She dared to take a shallow, relieved breath. Moving, on the other hand, wasn't in her immediate future, at least for the next couple of minutes.

Tilting her head, she spied Ennis leaned over the edge about ten feet above her. He yelled down, "You okay?"

"I'm alright!" she replied. At least she hoped she was. Her leg ached but she figured cold and tension from the fall caused it.

Upon hearing her response, Ennis leaned over the precipice to ensure she heard, "Damn it, woman! When I get my hands on you, you'll wish you'd have listened!"

Staring down into the white abyss, unsure of the footholds going down, she yelled back, "Promises, promises!"

"Stay put and don't move! I'll get my rope and pull you up!"

What, by the neck? She'd never heard her partner so spitting mad at her. Savannah tilted her head back but Ennis had gone to fetch the rope. She took a tentative step and sighed when the foothold was solid. Another step to the side and it too proved solid. Slowly and carefully she inched her way down until Monty's snow covered coat was nearly within reach. She called his name while venturing down to alert him someone was there *and* to drown out Ennis's curses from above. So far he'd threatened to keelhaul her, tar and feather her, drag her back home over his horse's back, and the coup de grace: "I'm putting your pretty ass over my knee and you ain't gettin' up until it's red as an apple!"

Despite his lofty plans or her argument against them, she needed to help Monty first. "Monty!" she shouted again. This time she was close enough her hand brushed the back of his coat but the boy remained motionless in the mounded snow.

Savannah cautiously stepped her way to the bottom where she stood knee deep in snow. She welcomed the semi-calm from the storm, especially for Monty's sake. The wind blew gale force above but in the yawning trench the speeds reduced to manageable except when it gusted. The snow swirled down the wall, blasting her in the face with painful snowflakes.

Closer to the wall it drifted over three feet deep but Monty had huddled in the middle where the snow wasn't as deep. Still, it covered him from head to toe except one small area of his coat and a light dusting on his face and dark hair. His Stetson sat a few feet away, practically buried in snow. Had he tripped and fallen into the small canyon as she had? If so, did he suffer injuries from it? There was a reason the boy curled up in the storm instead of fighting it to get home. She hated to move him for fear of further injury but leaving him to freeze wasn't exactly an alternative either.

Savannah kneeled down to scoop the accumulated snow from Monty's body. She brushed the layer of snow from his face and found his collar flipped up to block the snow from his face.

She repeatedly called his name, hoping he'd respond. Panic set in when he remained stone quiet. Slipping off her glove, she reached in his coat to feel for a pulse. His neck was cool, nearly cold, but she felt a strong pulse against her fingertips. Before moving him, she carefully dug the snow from around his head, searching for injuries or blood. Thankfully she found none. "Ennis!" she shouted, "I need the blankets!"

Ennis cupped his ear, "What?"

Taking his lead, she cupped her hands around her mouth, "The blankets!" She saw him nod then disappear. Only seconds passed when he reappeared holding the blankets they'd packed for Monty. He tossed them down one at a time, three total. Savannah unfolded one and laid it across the boy. While she worked with the second, Ennis yelled, "How is he?"

She responded with her findings with emphasis on Monty's strong pulse. Each second he lay in the snow drained his body heat. Savannah dug the snow from around the child then wrapped the second and third blankets over him. Reaching down, she told Monty, "I hope this is the right thing to do, sweetheart. I have to get you warm somehow. I'm just hopin' you're not injured anywhere."

She curled her arms beneath his body, hoisted him into her embrace with his head resting on her shoulder. Savannah positioned the top blanket over his head to help shield his face from blowing snow. She snuggled him close, "Monty, sweetheart, wake up." She spoke softly while letting her body heat try to warm him. The frigid cold sank deep to her bones and shivers raked over her. She spent less time in the weather than Monty so she could only imagine how frozen he felt.

She adjusted the blankets until they provided a snug cocoon around him, "Monty," she pleaded, "open your eyes for me. Show me you're okay."

The faintest movement of his lips spurred her to continue talking him awake. Slowly, it seemed, the boy regained consciousness. Savannah hugged him to her, willing her body to transfer the needed heat to Monty. A small sound finally came from him, "Mama?"

"Honey, it's Savannah. You scared us all half to death. Everyone's looking for you. Uncle Ennis and I finally found you." A sudden tsunami of snow cascaded down the wall, startling her and forcing her to turn to protect Monty's face. Ennis appeared from behind the wave, "How is he?"

"Waking up. Oh," she mentioned offhandedly, "and I want nothing more said about *me* sliding down that wall, Mr. Avalanche."

Ennis pursed his lips but took it well, "The boys are coming. Then we can all get out of here, go home and get warm." He rubbed his hands together, cupped them around his mouth to blow warmth into them, "Is there room for a third person?"

She nodded, "Three's never a crowd with us. Climb on in."

Ennis huddled close to the pair, wrapped his arms around them, "Monty, your mama and daddy are real happy to know you're okay. Cal's on his way to take you home."

"Savannah found me," he whispered and pulled his arms from under the blankets and hugged her neck.

"Yes, she did," Ennis replied with a generous amount of pride. His gentle smile and Monty's embrace caused tears to well in her eyes. The boy hugged her with every bit of strength he had. She returned the hug, "You gettin' warm yet, baby?"

He nodded slightly, his eyes closing. Savannah cautioned, "You have to stay awake, Monty. You can sleep later, okay?" His little nod warmed her heart as he snuggled against her. She looked at Ennis, "He's a sweetheart."

"We try to grow 'em that way," he replied just before a wind-driven cloud of snow whipped around them. The infinitesimal flakes stung like needles in her skin. Both she and Ennis hunched their shoulders against the wind to protect their faces.

Savannah finally figured out what a cowboy hat was good for – blocking the wind and snow. "How far out were your brothers?" she asked, hating to raise her voice. Then she realized it was probably best they speak loudly so Monty didn't drop off asleep.

Ennis shrugged, "Dunno. They'll be here shortly though." He turned his face to the other shoulder, finishing, "I hope." He'd said it under his breath but the wind diminished just enough she heard every syllable. Without furthering it, she suggested, "If they don't show soon, we'll need to find a way out ourselves."

Ennis barely nodded. He looked away and she knew he dreaded the possibility. The idea didn't set well with her either but between that or freezing to death, she'd hike those few miles home, especially if it saved Monty.

The boy's strength gradually returned as she and Ennis stood with him between them, a little Monty Rutherford sandwich. "How do you get him to the hospital in this weather?" she inquired.

He gave the surroundings a brief glance, "Don't know that we can. Roads are closed. Mama knows a doctor so she'll call him for advice."

"I don't know if he's hurt but it's so cold I'm not sure he could feel it if he was."

"I'm okay," Monty's soft voice assured. "Just cold." He reinforced his hold around her neck and for the first time in a long while, the longing to have a child resurfaced. It appeared on rare occasion, usually around Seth's kids and it hadn't shown itself in quiet a while. Today, it magnified to a genuine desire as Monty's small arms hugged her close.

Savannah chanced a look up but saw no sign of the brothers. Her body continued to shiver even snuggled against Ennis. She noticed his vision trained on her. To pass the time, she asked, "Ennis, are you going to tell your family about us?"

"I'd rather not. They've all fallen in love with you. Seems kinda mean to tell them after that. They've got it in their minds we're going steady so –"

"They think we're *engaged*, Ennis. That's way different than going steady. We need to let them know we're not getting married."

The decision didn't set well and he huffed through pursed lips, "Yeah, okay."

His mood clearly spiraled downward until a brutal gust of wind shattered the tense moment. Ennis tried to put his back to the wind, "Let's get Monty through this first." He called on his nephew, "How you doing, squirt?" The answer sounded muffled, even to Savannah. She adjusted her hold to stir him, "Monty? You still awake?"

"M-hmm," he answered. His hold grew sluggish, though, and it concerned her. It seemed like a lifetime passed since they found the boy. Her body now trembled of its own volition, and her teeth chattered. She asked Ennis the time. He quickly referenced his watch, "It's been twenty minutes since I let them know we found Monty." He dug in his coat for the walkie-talkie and attempted to contact his brothers. Cutting his vision to her, he asked, "You okay?"

"I will be soon as I get warm."

A steady hum of static rattled from the handheld's speaker. Ennis pocketed the unit and wrapped her in a tighter embrace, "Once we get home, I promise to get you so hot you'll beg for air conditioning."

Savannah gifted him with a small, quivering smile. He had a heart of gold and a reach a mile long. She swore his arms curled completely around her and Monty, enveloping them in a loving and, she was sure, warm embrace. If only she could feel it...

He leaned closer to her ear, "If they aren't here in five minutes, we'll head out on our own. We just need to find a way up then we can ride on home."

She closed her eyes and pictured the fireplace back at the Rutherford house. The crackling logs, the yellow and orange flames flickering back and forth. She vowed to roost there until the New Year or until she could feel her toes again, whichever came first.

A bellowing holler came from above while a distinct hiss emanated from the walkie-talkie. It sputtered to life again, this time with Cal's voice calling for Ennis, "We're dropping ropes for you then we'll let the horses help pull you out. Send Savannah up first."

Ennis responded only to see sheer terror in his partner's eyes. Before backpedaling entirely, Savannah wanted to know, "Exactly how does this theory work? Without injuring someone greatly, I mean?"

From the corner of her vision she saw two ropes fly down and whip against the wall of snow. She wasn't in the marines or army so climbing her way up wasn't feasible but she *really* didn't want a horse in charge of her wellbeing either.

Ennis explained as best he could but the trepidation remained in her features, "How do we get Monty out?"

"I'll carry him while the boys pull me up."

"No," another voice argued. Monty held tighter to Savannah's neck, "I want Savannah to take me."

The two adults stared at each other. The remark stunned them but Ennis found his voice quickly, "Sorry, buddy, but I promise you can ride home with her. That'll give you plenty of time together."

Monty held tighter around her neck but nodded anyway. In her heart she didn't like the decision either however her brain concluded Ennis did the right thing. She wasn't accustomed to being towed with a rope – especially with a horse on the other end. Carrying a child at the same time wasn't entirely prudent. She debated about asking a particular question because this feat sounded too unbelievable, "Have you actually attempted this stunt before? Pulling people out of canyons with a horse and a rope?"

"Couple of times, yeah."

"And no one was killed or maimed in the process?"

Ennis smiled easily, "Trust me, sweetheart. Since we *will* get married some day, I don't want anything happening to my future wife."

"Okay," she frowned good-naturedly, "*now* I'm scared. The cold is affecting your better judgment."

Even as the snow stung her skin and the bitter wind chilled her, Ennis's wink served as a hefty dose of warmth for her heart. He meant to marry her "come hell or high water" he'd said. Standing in the middle of nowhere in a raging blizzard, her heart sent a whimsical message to her brain – accept his proposal.

Without a moment to casually entertain the idea, she felt his hand at her back, directing her toward the chasm's wall. Ennis explained, "One of the boys will be on point, watching you. The other two will be working the horses. They don't want to hurt you anymore than you want to be hurt." They made their way to the two dangling ropes which, upon additional inspection, appeared rather meager for hauling individuals up a steep incline.

Her partner seemed to read her mind, "These ropes are strong enough. We rope calves with them so they'll hold ten of you."

Another wave of doubt washed over her. Now wasn't the time for flattery. The flimsy dangling ropes looked worn and weathered. She only needed them to hold one of her, not ten. She stared at the ropes like a vertigo victim about to skydive, "I'll need guidance."

"And I'll need Monty." They made the transfer smoothly, even with Monty's objections. Ennis held the boy much like she had only with more ease. She stretched her arms which finally informed her how tired they were. She hadn't noticed until Ennis took the child. Now they felt empty and shaky.

Ennis grabbed one lasso and shook out the loop to widen it, "Lift your arms again."

"So it *doesn't* go around my neck after all," she joked.

He slid the loop down around her until it fit snug beneath her arms. He pulled it taut but not hard, "I still owe you for earlier. You could have killed yourself."

Savannah presented her own wink at her partner, "Good luck following through with any of those promises you mentioned."

Ennis winked back, a sly grin spreading, "Oh, I have the perfect one in mind for you. And in this weather, escaping isn't an option."

The temptation to daydream about his "threat" took a serious back seat when he tugged the rope and spoke into the walkie-talkie, "Give us thirty seconds and you can start." Ennis handed her the second rope, "Hold it to help guide you. Just pretend you're rock climbing without footholds."

A nervous smile trembled across her lips, "Something I always wanted to do." Savannah tilted back, surveying the climb ahead of her. It might as well have been the Grand Canyon to her but after taking a deep breath, she nodded, "Piece of cake, right?"

He nodded, "Chocolate cake with ice cream."

Checking her hold on the guide rope, she corrected, "I'll skip the ice cream until I'm warmer." Before the brothers began lifting her, she warned Ennis to step back, "I don't want you or Monty buried in snow if this stuff gives way."

He waved an acknowledgment and stepped far back just as the rope tightened. Savannah gasped as the rope constricted around her chest and she wrapped the guide rope around her forearm to keep hold. Slowly she ascended the cliff, sinking one boot then the other into the drifted snow along the side. Fear of slipping lurked at the back of her mind and she prayed for solid footing the higher she climbed. She kept the rope firm around her arm to keep the stress off the lasso around her chest. She hadn't a clue how long the act took or how silly she looked during it, all she realized was the secure feeling of hands beneath her arms, pulling her the rest of the way up. Dane and Cal brought her to her feet as if she were weightless. "You okay, Peach?" Dane asked.

She nodded, visibly relieved, "Thanks for making it so easy."

"Our pleasure," he replied. "I guess your grandpa showed you how to climb too 'cause you shimmied up that wall like a monkey."

Cal tossed the rope down again, radioed to Ennis then thanked Savannah for finding Monty, "If you're this good, we may not let you go home. You'd make a hell of a rancher's wife."

She accepted it as the compliment it meant to be. Cal certainly knew what he was talking about, being the oldest running the ranch. Ennis explained all the boys learned ranch life from infancy but the other three were obsessed with it. He gave an honest effort but the lifestyle didn't "set with him". Why he chose law enforcement was a question she'd not discovered an answer for. He held her off the subject like she held him off the details of her childhood. Some things, she reflected, needed to be served in small doses when ventured into.

Savannah pushed the hat down on her head. The wind still howled and shot snow horizontally like tiny arrows. Feeling the sting in her ears, she pulled the coat collar up again. "Anything I can do to help?" she called over the wind.

Both Cal and Dane shook their heads. She saw Cal give Jake a signal she took to mean "slow down" and the horse basically stopped.

The youngest brother watched intently for signals given at regular intervals. Dane busied himself with the other horse, he too watched his brother for signals. Dane worked the guide rope and Savannah noticed as she'd climbed, she felt little slack in it but it remained taut enough to keep her steady. Jake worked the rope around Ennis's chest. She'd noticed with him also that he'd kept the rope taut but allowed her to use her feet on the incline. Initially she anticipated a horribly painful trip up the side. What she got was a climbing lesson with two lassos as her safety net. Not nearly as nightmarish as originally imagined.

Suddenly Ennis came into view, his head poking up over the edge. She saw pure determination and strength in action. One arm supported Monty while the other used the guide rope. Monty huddled beneath the blankets – he looked relaxed and peaceful like a trip up a canyon wall was a daily occurrence.

Dane transported Monty from Ennis's arms to Savannah, "I understand you're his ride home."

Monty grabbed around her neck with a vehemence of a lost child finding his mother. Savannah hugged him close and smiled at Dane, "As you said, it's my pleasure."

11

They rode thirty minutes and the house still remained somewhere obscured by the blizzard's wind and blowing snow. Savannah was grateful her companions knew the land. Had she embarked by herself, the Rutherfords would have two people to search for instead of one. The surrounding area resembled a giant white blanket with barbed wire fences for stitching. Discerning even ground from a rise or dip became impossible. Their horses began to suffer as they plodded along. They seemed equally as exhausted with the travels as she. With snowflakes on their manes and tails and snow pelting their sides, the beasts huffed and puffed their way diligently to give their riders safe passage.

The layers of blankets tucked about him along with the gentle lumbering of the horses relaxed Monty in Savannah's hold. She'd settled the boy in front of her on the saddle, his arms still tight around her neck. Riding along, she kept an arm securely around him while guiding the horse with her free hand.

Less than five minutes into the ride home, Dane pointed at her leg, "You got a problem, Peach."

Ennis hurried his horse around to hers, his attention following his brother's pointing finger. He grimaced, "I knew that fall looked dangerous."

Savannah detected the overbearing Ennis emerging judging from his tone. His only highly aggravating trait barreled to the forefront with no signs of braking. The scowl he wore could have terrified demons. His dark eyes flicked up to her already blossoming warning look then returned to the bleeding wound. She turned away, rolled her eyes. Ennis formulated a whopper of a lecture at times which produced a heartfelt sympathy from her toward his future children. After a lengthy, exhaustive lecture and subsequent first aid, they'd receive a sermon of how to prevent such things from happening again.

She angled her leg to examine it. A sizeable splotch of blood spread on the jeans just below her knee. The cold essentially numbed the wound but at times an intermittent dull stinging reminded her she somehow screwed up. The injury's severity certainly didn't necessitate the current frown it received from Ennis. "It's nothing," she tried to calm him down. "I'll just clean it when I get to the house."

Ennis pulled alongside her, his expression matching Dane's brow for brow, wrinkle for wrinkle, "*I'll* clean it when we get there. Then I can judge just how hard to spank you for defying me."

She noticed Dane broke into a grin as he steered his mount away from the conversation. "Ennis, you try that and I'll hurt you." With her declaration, she witnessed Dane steer back to them. Evidently no one wrangled with a Rutherford – until now.

Ennis and Savannah stared the other down until Cal rode beside his brother, "Leave her alone. Just be glad it's her leg and not her head."

"You're telling me you wouldn't go nuts if Bobbi hurt herself?"

"Of course I would but we've both got strong-headed women. If I treated my wife like you're treating Savannah, Bobbi'd chase me down until she sufficiently walloped me upside the head."

Ennis slanted his partner a questioning glance. Savannah smiled a little. Cal understood more about women than she imagined. Being the only married brother, she figured he'd learned the hard way more times than not. He tried to educate Ennis and she appreciated his gentle approach. She didn't mind her partner looking after her to a point but growing up as she had, taking care of herself came naturally – having a man do it stripped every gear in her brain.

Cal leaned nearer, raised his voice over the howling wind, "Ennis, here's some advice for a happier marriage. Unless she mentions lighting herself on fire, you'd best keep your mouth shut. Believe me, a woman's anger lasts ten times longer than a man's."

Ennis hunkered down to mentally chew on the words. Several seconds passed when he finally capitulated. "I'm still cleaning that wound. I won't hear another word of it."

They rode for another fifteen minutes until finally arriving home. Bobbi darted out the back door, arms open wide for Monty, her face streaked with joyful tears unlike the last time Savannah saw her. Lifting the boy down to his mother, a distinct loneliness swept over Savannah. For the past hour or more, she and Monty developed a special bond. Now her arms felt empty, the contentment of a child clinging to her for comfort was gone. She watched as Monty threw his arms around his mother's neck much like he had hers earlier. Then she smiled at the unmistakable joy both displayed of their reunion.

"I'll help you down," Ennis called beside her. Reminiscent of the boy's actions, her partner's arms reached for her. This time she'd take the help.

Savannah swung her wounded leg over the horse's back at the same time Ennis's large hands planted themselves on her waist. With his strength, her feet touched the ground so gently, she barely felt it.

He curled his arm around her to help support her, "I'll carry you to the bathroom and clean that wound –"

"Ennis, I'm fine. There's no need to carry me anywhere." With her statement, she felt his hand compress lightly on her hip. She didn't exactly care if she ticked him off. He treated her as if the leg was broken instead of having a small cut.

"Savannah, stop being so bull-headed. I'm carrying you and that's –"

"Ennis," Cal interrupted. He tapped his Stetson against his knee to knock the snow off. Once he gained his brother's line of vision, he finished, "Remember what Pa said. Never miss a good chance to shut up. Let her walk and she *might* let you tend to that cut."

Again she saw her partner battle against his protective nature. Finally, he shrugged, yielding to his older brother's advice. Savannah started toward the bathroom and chanced a glimpse over her shoulder. Ennis appeared positively deflated with defeat.

He was raised to be chivalrous, to take care of women, she reminded herself. He was only trying to help. No matter how independent she presented herself, he would at least offer.

"Ennis," she called, a grimace narrowing her eyes. The pain wasn't debilitating but the warm house awakened the nerves considerably. Mostly guilt ate at her. Guilt for calling him down and hurting his feelings. She waved him over, "Help me to the bathroom?"

With the exception of "Yes, I'll marry you", Savannah doubted any combination of syllables pleased him more. Two long strides later found him beside her, his arm snug around her waist.

Her father always taught that reliance on another person for any reason promoted weakness. He instilled that belief with words and fists. She found it interesting that R.J. preached his beliefs while beating independent thoughts and actions out of his children. The remembrance prompted memories of Ennis's feather touch along the scars on her back. His fingers trembled while tracing R.J.'s handiwork. She sensed the rage building inside him, heard his unspoken questions. Explaining that part of her childhood had to wait. She was neither ready to verbalize the painful memories nor did she believe Ennis was prepared to hear them.

Savannah leaned into Ennis, her arm hugging him tighter. No matter what her father said, reliance on another person – if it's the right person – could be a beautiful thing.

A certain degree of visible pride poured off her partner. She figured part of it revolved around getting his way, the other that Savannah proved Cal wrong, at least a little. Ennis helped her to the bathroom and lifted her onto the cabinet, "Is it hurting pretty good?"

"I've had worse but it's beginning to ache a bit."

He closed the door, set the lock then cleared his throat uneasily, "You'll have to take off those jeans, you know."

"I kinda presumed I might," was her casual response. He seemed more ill at ease with her undressing than she was. He nervously looked one way then the other in the small bathroom as if searching for a safe way out.

She shrugged from the coat first. She lifted her sweatshirt enough to reveal the top button of her jeans. Ennis busied himself by removing his coat. The instant he turned to see her unbuttoning the jeans, his attention riveted to the sight, evidently mesmerized by the action. By the last button, he'd seen her lavender panties. Savannah noticed his cheeks slashed with color and the beginnings of perspiration formed on his face. The temperature inside roused the blood in her extremities, making them tingle. Her fingers and toes telegraphed their presence with every heartbeat. If the heat in the house caused Ennis to break such a sweat, she needed to toss him in a snow drift.

Without removing his vision from her panties, he cleared his throat again. The action failed to rid the coarseness from his voice, "I'll help with your boots."

"Thanks," she sighed. Getting those off would help immensely. Her feet swelled in them, and her ankles felt like softballs. She hopped onto the cabinet, inadvertently presenting Ennis a biblical temptation. Even as he pulled the cowboy boots off, his vision occasionally strayed to her panties. She found it amusing, "Something wrong, Ennis?"

"Nope," he croaked. He leaned in for a solid grasp of the boot's heel which brought his head closer to his temptation. Like a gentleman, he turned away but she noticed he found it difficult. Once her jeans slipped off, she reached down and tenderly smoothed his hair. Between the cowboy hat and wind it had gone askew and she combed it into place, noticing how soft it felt beneath her touch, "You're not too mad, are you?"

Ennis swallowed hard, leaned into her touch as she caressed behind his ear. His eyes leisurely closed, he took a long, deep breath. Savannah threaded her fingers through his hair. His dark eyes slowly opened, centered directly on hers. There was no mistaking his feelings or emotions. "I was scared," his rough voice confessed. "Scared you'd hurt yourself or worse. But I'm not mad."

"Good," she whispered. "I don't like it when you're mad at me."

Ennis's gaze lowered to her lips. His desire ultimately surfaced, "God, I want to kiss you."

Her hand urged him up. Truth was she wanted him to kiss her. One of those long, knee-weakening kisses he'd gifted her with before. She wanted to feel his lips on hers, wanted to taste him, wanted to feel his passion. With a simple kiss, he stole her stability, both emotional and physical. As if he read her mind, Ennis rose, cupped her face in his palms. The instant their lips met, a tingle worked from her lips downward to her toes. Ennis gave her little time to react before thrusting his tongue inside, hungrily exploring. The forceful kiss initially shocked her but she quickly settled into it, her tongue joining his in its own ravenous exploration. The rasp of his beard sent a shiver of excitement racing through her as she held him, her eyes drifting closed to feel all the sensations, his texture and taste, his eagerness.

His fingers threaded her hair like hers had his. Ennis held her softly while ravishing her mouth to the point Savannah nearly forgot to breathe.

One hand dropped to her waist and Savannah felt his fingers splay across the small of her back as he drew her to him. His arousal pressed against her belly, begging for more than merely a sultry kiss.

A banging on the door startled them but Ennis slowly separated, his vision never straying from hers. "What?" he asked the intruder.

It was Dane, which surprised neither of them, "You finished playing doctor with Peach? Mama's got lunch about done."

"Be out shortly," Ennis left it at that and dove in for another kiss, this one even more fiery and unyielding than the last.

Savannah grew weak in his hold. She'd never been thoroughly kissed like this in her life. So forcefully yet gently.

"Ma, I think they're up to no good in there!" Dane called then chuckled so they undoubtedly heard him.

Ennis groaned. He pulled away but Savannah knew he hadn't wanted to. He was fuming mad at his brother and actually so was she. Dane tried every trick possible to tease and upset his brother. She put a hand to Ennis's chest, assuring, "We'll resume this kiss later. Away from your brother."

"You'll have to hold me back, sweetheart. I'm close to killing him right now." He knelt down and winced at the wound on her leg, "Cut it pretty good." After cleaning it with soap, he located the alcohol in the cabinet. Before pouring it over the wound, he forewarned, "Try not to kick me."

She winked, "I'm saving that for Dane."

12

Mama Rutherford prepared a hefty, filling lunch for the brood. Ennis watched his partner's jaw drop at the sight of the table brimming with everything from steaks to creamed potatoes, corn, green beans and homemade rolls. He tried to tell Savannah that Georgia and his mother shared a lot in common. Georgia baked cakes and brownies when stressed out. His mother tackled the main course. He was convinced that if the two ever shared a kitchen, they could easily put fifty pounds on any unsuspecting soul in less than a week.

Savannah wasn't used to eating so much or so often. The sheer amount of food stunned her at every turn and left her speechless when the serving dishes sat empty by meal's end. Ennis suspected a lot surprised his partner, not just the food. His family welcomed her as theirs which initially unsettled her. He noticed over the past week or so she'd relaxed quite a bit. His mother's impromptu hugs, his brothers' continual teasing and Bobbi's spunky personality were all accepted now, not shied from.

After he patched her leg, Savannah passed on eating for curling up in a rocker, covered with a cobalt blue blanket. Monty insisted she stay with him in the guest room where Bobbi socked him in bed, covered in his own collection of blankets.

Ennis couldn't eat either. He worried about his nephew and his partner. She'd gotten chilled pretty good during the search. The only time she stopped shivering was while they kissed. Hell, he'd give her a lifelong lip-lock if it kept her warm. Loving a woman any deeper was impossible. She knew he loved her. He knew she had feelings for him but he hesitated to call it love. Still, that kiss conveyed more than "I like you".

While the others ate, Ennis meandered to the bedroom door to see her sitting in a rocking chair, the blanket covering her from toe to chin. She resembled a young girl rocking herself to sleep. Her cheeks faded from scarlet to pink since they came in from the storm. As she rocked, her eyes grew heavy-lidded from fatigue.

Monty lay under a mountain of blankets, his chafed little face looked weary and sleepy. When he spoke, Savannah came wide awake to reply. She encouraged the boy to close his eyes and rest. The youngster's eyes blinked lazily a few times then closed.

After a couple of minutes, Savannah rose from the rocker and folded the blue blanket over her arm. Ennis smiled at the sight of her readjusting Monty's covers and sweeping a lock of hair aside to place a kiss on the boy's forehead. She stood, stretched, and turned to see the grin on her partner's face. "What?" she whispered.

He shook his head and shrugged, "Nothin'. You're just good with kids, that's all." Before giving her time to deny it, he asked, "You gonna eat lunch?"

Savannah hesitated then shook her head, "Not really hungry. It's been quite an extraordinary morning."

"Turned out good, though."

"Turned out better than good. Are you eating lunch?"

Ennis leaned in, his lips brushing her ear, "Personally, I'd like to recommence that kiss we started." He wasn't sure but he thought he detected a glimmer in her blue eyes when she looked at him. A short few seconds passed when she removed all doubt by lifting to tip-toe, answering, "Me too."

They braved the snow once more, this time to retreat to the little ranch house. They sheltered their horses in the nearby stable then trudged through the snow until they stood in the warmth of the tiny house.

The cold ride promoted thoughts of hot showers instead of kissing – at least for the meantime. Savannah partook of a hot, relaxing shower, threw on her pajamas and piled up in the bed. In the meantime, Ennis migrated to the space heater to warm his hands and other extremities. He watched her yank the covers to her chin like she'd done in Monty's room, "Need some extra body heat?"

"Whenever you're ready."

Those normally innocent words brewed a storm below his belt that threatened to shame the one raging outside. Ennis grimaced as his pants grew smaller thanks to an overanxious erection. He was ready anytime when it concerned Savannah. All he required was an invitation – and she'd just gifted him with one. He unbuckled his belt, "I'll grab a quick shower and be right there." Ennis zipped the belt through the loops, threw it to the couch then frantically fumbled with the buttons on his jeans. "Hold that thought."

A smile curved Savannah's lips. Sometimes Ennis was funnier when he didn't intend to be. His fingers were a blur while working the jeans open like his crotch was on fire. He shucked the denim and had stepped out of them before thinking to close the bathroom door behind him. The image brought a chuckle from her. Comical or not, Ennis always made her smile.

He took a quicker shower than she. To her surprise the door opened a few minutes later – or what she guesstimated as a few. A small cloud of steam billowed out and Ennis peeked around the door, "Still holding that thought?"

"With both hands."

"Good," he responded, stepped into the room. Savannah could do nothing but blatantly stare since he emerged from the bathroom wearing only boxers. A million words flew harum-scarum in her head, all relating to the sexy male before her. Sorting through them to create a lick of sense proved futile. She'd seen Ennis without a shirt and each time the temptation grew to colossal proportions but to behold the man in this near naked state, she couldn't even swallow correctly, much less speak. Dragging her vision from his sculpted male form either took a miracle or a good slap. Still owl-eyed, she inquired, "Aren't you freezing?"

"Actually," he replied, his voice rough, "the scenery is pretty hot so I'm okay."

No kidding, she wanted to say. From her point of view the scenery was hotter than Atlanta in mid-July. Seeing Ennis standing beside the bed, his broad chest liberally sprinkled in dark curls, she really wouldn't object to him wrapping himself around her. Or vise versa, for that matter. She visually explored his physique from his damp hair down his strong arms and chest. The thick hair on his chest trailed toward his wide shoulders then dove like an arrow down his belly and disappeared into his boxers. One giant hunk of gorgeous male – that was Ennis Rutherford. And after that blazing kiss they shared in the bathroom, there was no looking at the man the same way again.

Ennis didn't move, "You comfortable with how I'm dressed?"

When she nodded, he rounded the other side and slid beside her. Savannah closed her eyes but the same images kept creeping in – hell, they *danced* in. When she turned on her side, she felt him snuggle against her back, intensifying the fantasy swirling in her brain. His leg eased over hers and his arm hugged her close. Feeling trapped never felt so good, so perfect… His fingers intertwined with hers, "This feels really nice."

"Yes, it does," she agreed. She didn't trust herself to say anything further. However subtle the words, the meaning would unquestionably emerge as "I want you, right here, right now." Of course Ennis's lower half made a similar statement. When he snuggled closer, Savannah noticed he had another substantial boner and it pressed tenaciously against her bottom. "Ennis?"

He drew a long, deep breath, "M-hmm." Whether he chose not to mention it or mistakenly assumed she couldn't feel it, she didn't know. She *did* know his nose now made itself at home with her hair. "Is there something we need to discuss?" she asked.

"You mean how I've suffered blue balls since we met and how I'd give my right arm to cure them?"

His candor surprised but flattered her. It was the first time he'd been so direct with her about sex and his announcement took a moment to soak in. When it did, a tiny smile curved her lips – a smile he couldn't see, "Something like that, yeah."

She half-expected him to move his hand, his leg, anything. He remained so still she felt his heartbeat against her back, "It's no secret that I have feelings for you. I'd be certifiably dumb or gay not to be attracted to you."

Savannah chuckled, encouraging him to cuddle closer. His erection nestled itself at home at her backside – obviously it was staying nice and cozy. "Tell you a secret?" she asked.

"Sure."

"I'm attracted to you too."

Ennis groaned the sound of a man relieved but in sincere discomfort. He kissed her, "Ever thought about doing something about it?"

Her thumb stroked his knuckles, "It's shameful how often I do but I've never slept with a co-worker, especially not a partner. As I've heard things have a tendency to go haywire."

Ennis retrieved his hand, brushed her hair back and he pressed a soft kiss to her neck, "They don't have to. I've never felt this way before. These feelings are new to me but I do know I'd die before hurting you."

Savannah felt herself momentarily stiffen. He had the tone of a man wanting to slap a brand on her, or at least a ring. Ennis evidently read her mind, "I'm only talking the commitment of two people who care about each other." He pressed another kiss, a slow gentle one at her shoulder. "I'll make you a deal," he offered. "If we end up throwing things at each other, I'll transfer to Zone 3."

She laughed softly, "Is that your definition of punishment or what?"

He kissed behind her ear, outwardly delighting in the tremulous breath she drew. He smiled against her skin, replying, "Any place away from you is punishment." Ennis held her even closer, "I was so afraid of losing you today. You tumbled into that gully and my heart stopped."

"I slid, Ennis. I didn't tumble."

To hush her, he planted another little kiss beneath her ear, "It looked like a dangerous fall to me."

Savannah leisurely turned on her back. Looking into her partner's eyes she saw lust deeper than the snow outside but not just lust alone. She'd have sworn love danced in them. That, along with his tender touch and concern tugged at a part of her she'd closed off for years. She really didn't want to love Ennis. Love complicated friendship, snarled and tangled it into a mess neither person could unravel. Then, out of the blue, it inevitably unwound at lightning pace, leaving two lives shattered.

Looking in her partner's eyes, she felt herself falling fast, her heart giving what she'd protected for many years. In his warm gaze she found the promise to love her forever. A promise her head staunchly objected to – no one could vow to always love another, or they shouldn't. Promises were easily broken, hearts too.

Savannah touched his cheek, "I can't believe you said you loved me." It lingered in her mind since he'd spoken the words. She refused to wholly believe him until... Well, until now. She spent her life retreating from men who said the word "love" simply because it only meant "sex". They "loved" her for her looks or what she could do for them. Love never meant sharing their lives, celebrating the good times and sticking around for the hard ones. It never meant growing old together. Not until she met Ennis...

Ennis didn't verbally retreat or apologize for declaring his feelings. Instead, he nodded, "I do love you. I want to hold you, kiss you and cherish you every day. I want to make love to you until you surrender your stubborn streak about loving me. I'm the son of a Texas rancher who loved one woman until he died and I'm just like my father. You're my one and only and I'll love you till my last breath. Even in death I'll love you. If that scares you, I can't help it. That's the God's honest truth."

Normally, Savannah's body and mind worked as a symphony to flee such a declaration. Now, however, she found herself battling tears. She loved him too but disclosing it equated to breaking three hundred mirrors. It was a sure way to ruin their lives. She dared not say it, not yet.

Ennis's hand glided up then down the curve of her waist. He

patiently waited for a response or reaction. Besides sexy, patient described Ennis to a tee. In a perfect world, she'd declare her love for him, leaving the story with a happy ending. In her world, Ennis would have to be patient a little longer. Savannah smiled at last, her fingers curling behind his neck, "Break my stubborn streak."

Ennis's demeanor slowly transformed from cautious tension to unreserved passion. The declaration aroused him beyond her wildest dreams and she barely had time to breathe before he dove in for a kiss. He devoured and plundered her mouth with a ferocity that scattered all reason. In her life Savannah never experienced a wholly consuming kiss but she turned Ennis loose, gave him permission to break her mulishness. She hadn't realized he aimed for total surrender with one kiss. At this rate, she'd be boneless by midnight.

His hand still traced her side, his thumb brushed her taut nipple. Preventing her moans became pointless as he tormented the nub of flesh. She pushed her breast into his palm while threading her fingers through his thick hair. As they kissed, their tongues twirled and danced together and Ennis, showing his mischievous side, gently pinched her nipple. He smiled against her lips when she moaned again, arching into him.

His cool fingers slid beneath the pajama top, caressing her bare flesh. In her heart, Savannah was a total goner. Ennis's touch, his words, his spirit won her over months ago. She'd just been too damn hard-headed to admit it. Her heart finally gave her permission to love Ennis, no matter how her brain protested.

Regardless of her heart's decision, when he slid his hand along her hip and his fingers slipped inside her panties, a tiny siren began wailing at the back of her mind. Through the heady fog of shameless passion, it screamed its way to the forefront like the sex police and nearly bolted her upright in the bed. She pulled away from their fiery kiss, breathlessly inquiring, "Please tell me you have a condom."

Losing the connection of her kiss about sapped the life from him. She was there one minute, gone the next, leaving him struggling to catch his breath – and his hearing *and* common sense. He could have sworn he'd heard the word "condom" fall out of her mouth. He was hard as marble, his arousal basically begging to slide home and that word ground the amorous moment to an abrupt halt.

"What?" was all that squeaked out. Condom? No, of course he didn't have a condom, probably because he hadn't dreamed of actually scoring with Savannah Prince in the next century. Now in the middle of a damn blizzard, locked in a remote ranch house, horny as a kid on prom night she demanded a condom.

She rephrased it, "Do you have any protection?"

Aw, hell... He dare not move or express any emotion. One slip and Savannah would know the truth. His passion-laden brain scrambled for an answer. Finally it stumbled on, "Aren't you on the Pill?"

Her brow crinkled slightly between her eyes like she couldn't believe he'd ask, "Yes, but we need extra protection. I don't want babies right now, not with my career."

Of course not, he inwardly slapped himself. If she wasn't caving to marriage, she'd sure balk at having kids.

"Ennis, we can put this off. If you don't –"

"No," his voice sounded like thunder in his ears. Evidently it sounded the same to her because she pressed back into the pillow. His trembling fingers traced the line of her hair and he forced himself to calm down, "We're not delaying this, sweetheart. If I have to hike to town for a box, I will."

She propped on her elbows, clearly conveying her opinion that he'd lost every shred of his faculties, "In this weather? Ennis, you'll freeze to death. It's worse than this morning. The snow's deeper and the temperature's dropping."

Ennis balled his fists, disgusted at his forgetfulness, "I want you."

"I want you too but hospitals frown on fornication in the rooms. If you go traipsing around out there, you'll catch your death."

So many emotions and sensations coursed through his body he couldn't pinpoint anything but lust. She was there, waiting for him. She was *ready*.

He shoved a hand through his hair, spun on his heel and stalked to the bathroom. Once inside, he closed the door and shucked his shorts. His erection sprung forth with eagerness and an enthusiasm that frustrated him further. Obviously his hard-on hadn't received the news. There was no sex tonight. He seriously contemplated calling his brothers and pleading just one condom from them. Then a lone seed of rational thought sprouted into his conscious mind. *If you beg one from your brothers, you might as well tell Mama what you're doing because they will…*

Ennis gritted his teeth so hard his jaw ached. Life wasn't fair, he lamented while lightly banging his forehead against the wall. No, life was utterly hateful. Between it and fate, he might as well close up shop with the female population and become a monk.

There came a soft knocking at the door, "Ennis? Are you going to be okay?"

No, not unless someone put him out of his misery and quick. If boners could kill, he'd be dead a million times over. Their frequency increased ever since he laid eyes on the Southern beauty standing outside the door.

Ennis stared in the mirror, wondering what in his twenty-seven years he'd done to deserve this. He avoided black cats crossing his path nor did he walk under ladders, he regularly gave to charity and he read his Bible whenever possible.

Well, it didn't matter now, did it? Since a good roll in the hay had been cancelled due to his lack of foresight, he wished for the inadequate substitute of a good, stiff drink. To top off his lovely evening, he finally remembered the cupboards were bare – a circumstance he should have anticipated judging from his luck lately.

"Damn," he sighed, rubbing at the beginning headache in his temple. Ennis shook his head and resigned himself to belt back an aspirin with a sickeningly healthy drink of water.

Opening one drawer of the vanity, he rifled it roughly but thoroughly. Nothing. Next drawer. Nothing. Where the hell were the aspirin? His luck couldn't possibly be *that* bad, could it?

The next drawer he opened also appeared devoid of aspirin. However at the front of the drawer sat a note. He silently read it, "Do us a favor. Save the nieces and nephews until after the wedding." Dane's hen scratch served only to fuel his temper – until he looked beneath the note. His brother had placed a full box of brand new condoms in the vanity, probably knowing Ennis was a blockhead.

"Ennis? Did you hear me?" Savannah asked from behind the door.

Headache officially and magically eradicated now, he allowed a sinister grin to spread across his face as he opened the door. Savannah took a step back, leery of his expression. Her vision trekked downward and her blue eyes widened. His arousal received the message loud and clear: the mission was on again.

She stepped back again but Ennis met her step for step, the box hidden behind his back, "Take your clothes off."

"What?" her normally sultry tone lifted with surprise. Ennis watched her expression transform from registering shock to formulating a refusal.

His grin spread wider into a predatory one, "You heard me." He urged her backward again, "Take your clothes off."

She shook her head, visibly shoring up the remnants of her willpower, "It will tempt us to do something we shouldn't."

It tickled him to see her flustered. He'd seen the disappointment in her eyes and felt her body release the mounting tension they'd built in those few minutes. He backed her to the bed and smiled when she bumped the edge, lost her balance and bounced to the mattress – all without losing eye contact with him. Until... Her beautiful wide eyes returned to his erection, "You're really gonna have to fix that," she mumbled.

"I fully intend to," he agreed, his fingers threading her long hair and curling at the back of her head. He dove in for another kiss but this time Savannah placed her hands on his chest, stopping him. Ennis decided a little power play was in order. He engaged her in a forceful, take-no-prisoners lip-lock. He sat the box aside and allowed himself a gentle squeeze of her breast.

Gasping, Savannah parted from the kiss but he refused to stop thumbing her nipple. "Ennis, don't," she pleaded in a ragged breath. "I told you before, I'm only human."

He winked, "That's what I'm counting on." Then he nodded his head toward the box.

She glanced beside her left hip. Recognition only took a second and the words rolled off her tongue flavored with her gentle Georgia accent, "Why, you scoundrel."

"You ain't seen nothin' yet." He grasped her pajama top and removed it in one fluid movement. The sight of her breasts traveled straight down his body, his arousal lengthening in anticipation.

Savannah stared at it admiringly and also tinged with a hint of fear, "Exactly how big does it get?"

He bobbed his brow, "Let's find out." He tried to climb onto the bed but was again met with her hand to his chest.

"While we're finding out, let me attend to the protection. We don't want to be in the heat of the moment and forget."

Ennis closed his eyes at the mere suggestion of her touching him. He dreamt of this night so long, it required total concentration to keep his body's reaction under control. For a fleeting moment he entertained the notion of blocking her hand and putting the condom on himself. The desire to feel her touch overrode any protest his common sense might have provided.

He heard various sounds, box opening, the packet ripping, then her humorous declaration, "You look like I'm planning to hit you."

"Sorry," he answered in a tight, restrained tone, "just don't want to pull the trigger inadvertently."

"Would you rather attend to –"

"No," was all he said. It's all he could bring his conscious mind to say without losing his focus. Shortly after, it occurred to him that he'd sounded gruff. He gently amended, "I want you to."

Then he felt her. The touch went from stem to stern, softly first then she curled her hand around him. He moaned from deep in his chest, knowing he danced close to ruining the whole night. Ennis clenched his stomach – and anything else he could, "Houston, we'll have a problem if you don't hurry." She was driving him berserk with the gentle strokes.

"Our first time together and you want to blaze a trail," she teased. "What happened to the foreplay?"

Ennis released a long breath when she finally finished. "By the time I'm done with you, sugar," he promised, "you won't even remember your name."

13

If she ever doubted Ennis, he cured her of that. He kept his word and as she gradually regained some degree of consciousness, she managed to remember her name but nearly forgot where she was. When she oriented herself, she half-expected to find a wedding ring on her left hand. Ennis romped with the intensity of new groom, a groom possessing the staying power of the Energizer Bunny.

The cries of pleasure were so foreign to her that she was sure they raised the dead, not to mention his family down the road. At the time she didn't care if her own family heard them in Atlanta. Ennis sent her to places she only thought mythical *and* he hadn't worn out until the early morning hours.

She squinted to see his watch propped against the bedside lamp. The fact it was only nine o'clock *and* the fact breakfast was practically finished at the main house neglected to register in her haze of happiness. Surely after yesterday the whole family slept in, didn't they? At this rate, she'd be lucky to stay awake during the meal. Ennis left her positively boneless and exhausted.

Curling against him, she wondered why he wasn't already

married. If he exerted that same amount of patience and care with other women, a ring should have been neatly seated on his finger by now. Her skin tingled with memories of his touch. He touched every part of her sometimes so delicately it drove her mad. He certainly redefined the term "foreplay" but she also discovered he had a sadistic streak too. His large hands held her hips captive while he used his tongue to reduce her to begging. *Begging.* The mere recollection of it reddened her cheeks. She'd writhed and cried until capitulating to his one and only demand – that he take control that one night. At the time he sprung that little revelation on her, she was spent beyond sensible and conscious thought. Savannah violated her own rule and agreed to relinquish total control in the bedroom. It turned out to be the most blissful decision she'd ever made.

Savannah hugged her partner closer while reliving their night together. She placed a kiss on his bare shoulder, a small tender appreciation for his selfless ways. The few times she'd had sex, the man threw in a kiss, a grope and dove straight to the action. The experiences certainly couldn't be described as advertisements for fulfilling sex. Truthfully, she never saw the allure – until last night. Hugging him tighter, she felt her heart squeeze in her chest. Damn it all, she loved him. No matter how her brain warned her not to, she did anyway.

She kissed him again. This time Ennis drew a long, deep breath then turned in her embrace, a tired smile brightening his drowsy features, "Good morning."

"Good morning, stud."

Ennis brushed a wave of hair from her forehead, "You okay this morning?"

She snuggled in closer, "I'd say I'm pretty much perfect. And you?"

"Count me as perfect too." His large hand traced her back to her hip. When he urged her against him, her eyes widened in amazement, "Ennis?"

His smile evolved to a proud, albeit sleepy one, "Can't help myself."

His erection seemed eternal. He'd barely been awake a minute and he was hard as a rock again. Savannah recognized the sparkle in his dark eyes and the lilt in his voice…

The aroma of biscuits, gravy, eggs, and bacon wafted into Savannah's nose long before the group arrived at the house. As it were, Dane came knocking on their door shortly after they'd showered. He fell short of accusing or questioning their late arrival. Instead, he stood quietly, hands buried in his Arctic Drifter, waiting for her and Ennis to dress for the weather. Still feeling giddy from their activities, Savannah and Ennis slanted each other a secret smile behind his brother's back. Oh yes, coming to Texas turned out to be a splendid idea, she finally admitted.

Dane remained silent during the ride to the main house. By this time, both found it not only odd but disconcerting. "Dane, is something wrong?" she inquired.

"Oh," he drew the word out long and lazily, "that depends on the definition I put to that word."

"Something happened we need to know about?" Ennis questioned.

Dane's vision briefly shifted to his brother, "You know about it, brother. You *both* know about it."

The delivery of the statement hit with the delicacy of a hearty swing from a wooden baseball bat. Neither missed the inflection. Both chanced a glimpse of the other. Without words, they determined silence fit the moment better than ferreting out more information from Dane.

The trio reached the main house and dismounted, the only sounds being from the horses that seemed to sense the tension in their riders. "I'll tend to the horses," was all Dane said.

Savannah and Ennis stepped in the back door to shed their coats and boots. She didn't know about Ennis but despite his brother's mysterious irritable disposition, she was still ravenous. She planned on indulging in at least one huge plate full of Mama Rutherford and Bobbi's cooking. Only when the two entered the dining room, Savannah swore they all knew what transpired during the nighttime hours at the ranch house. The room fell silent, all eyes that pinned them finally drifted downward to their plates. Monty pouted, "'Bout time you guys showed up."

"They wouldn'ta showed up if Dane hadn'ta rousted 'em," Jake teased.

Every man in the dining room except Monty zeroed in on Mama Rutherford. She gave Ennis and Savannah a once over then smoothed her apron, "I'm with Monty. It's about time you showed up."

Savannah stood, mortified. The longer she and Ennis stood

before his family, the more she felt like a specimen. One of those two-headed pig or three-eyed frog specimens found at a carnival. Only the adults poked and tapped at the jar, not the kid.

She studied the expressions surrounding the table. While the men were reserved, the women appeared ready to bust about something. Their lips, especially Mama's, pursed as if trapping words behind them. It finally dawned on Savannah – they *all* knew about last night but weren't saying anything, probably for Monty's sake. The older woman nodded to two empty chairs placed together at the long dining table, "Let's eat."

Savannah slid in next to Monty and Ennis. The boy, suddenly chipper again, beamed from ear to ear when she sat down. He offered her his hand, "Got to do the prayer."

"Monty," Mama called, "would you do the honor once Dane arrives?"

That sounded pretty tense to me, Savannah noticed. Mrs. Rutherford was not pleased at all. With the airport closed for another day, the only alternative remained to stay quiet, keep a low profile. No one got in trouble if they kept their lips zipped. Then, when the friendly skies cleared and planes departed, so would she – as fast as humanly possible. Problem was she hated leaving Ennis behind to endure his family's interrogations and lectures. For her, the knowing looks and innuendo would be uncomfortable. For Ennis, it would be unbearable having to deal with his brother's incessant goading and teasing, and worst of all, his mother's disappointment. Because judging from Mama's expression, she definitely looked crushed.

Savannah heard the stomping of boots on the back door stoop. That particular someone attempted, like they all had, to remove the tons of snow stuck to their boots. The particular someone was Dane. He was back. *Yay.* Dane walked at a leisure pace then stopped in the dining room doorway – which happened to be directly behind Savannah. He waited a moment then, "Did they fess up yet?"

Cal stretched in his chair, "Nope. Mama's making 'em sweat it out."

"Calvin," Mama scolded. She told Dane to sit then Monty said a quick prayer, being sure to thank Savannah and Ennis for their help the day before. When Savannah felt Ennis's grasp on her hand tighten, she suddenly felt slightly better. Slightly. After a solid, "Amen!" from Monty, only Cal, Dane and Jake proceeded to attack the enormous layout of food presented on the table.

"Mama," Ennis asked, "is something wrong?"

His mother folded her hands in her lap, pensive about phrasing her thoughts, "I just wish you'd told us beforehand, that's all." She fidgeted with her napkin, creasing the corners then flattening them again, "I'm not *that* old fashioned, I don't think. I've always expected my boys to tell me anything."

Good thing Savannah wasn't eating at the time. She'd surely have either choked to her death or spewed like Vesuvius. Tell *his mother* what they were going to do? Either she slipped a cog or things were mighty different in Texas. It finally dawned on Savannah that his mother said "us". Mama wanted Savannah and Ennis to alert the entire family to their frolicking beforehand? The current moment rated as the most surreal and bizarre of Savannah's life. Last she remembered, making love fell into the category of not only spontaneous but private, not something couples announced to the media, much less their relatives. She trembled to think what his family planned to do *if* they had advance notice.

"What?" Ennis blurted, clearly thinking along the same lines as his partner.

Bobbi hadn't taken a bite of her meal yet, "We're all kinda hurt, Ennis. Didn't you trust us?"

"Well," Ennis dug into the bacon, stabbing two slices with his fork, "I can truthfully say Savannah and I hadn't entertained the thought of telling anyone in my family. Or hers, for that matter." He grabbed Savannah's fork and scooped up two slices of bacon for her also.

His words literally stunned the family into silence. Their hands halted in place, whether at their plates or their mouths. "Huh?" Cal grunted. He returned his fork back to the plate, "Lemme get this straight, little brother. You and Savannah were content on keeping *everyone* in the dark?"

"Well," now it was Savannah who spoke and uneasily at that, "it's not a subject my family is accustomed to discussing. None of us mentions it at all."

"You're kidding!" Bobbi exclaimed, her mouth agape.

Savannah's hand tightened on Ennis's. It was gonna get ugly, sure as she sat at the breakfast table breaking bread with them. It was gonna get down and dirty quick.

Cal's wife went through a plethora of expressions in a few short seconds. From utter shock it evolved to contemplation then settled on confusion. She frowned, "But aren't both your sister and brother married?"

"Yes, but they never forewarned me they were going to… Well, you know…" Awkwardness began to set in. She wanted to leave now, the fastest way possible. Ennis looked about the same way.

"Then how did you know they were doing it?" Jake looked harried. He stopped eating, his hands rubbed the back of his neck and he sighed. "How do you people live down there anyway? Do you even have telephones or running water?"

"Jacob," Mama scolded. At this rate, she'd call down every one at the table. Savannah just prayed she wasn't next.

Ennis, however, stood and proceeded to speed load both their plates with food, "That's it. We're eating in the living room then we're going back to the house for some peace and quiet."

"Sit down, young man," Mama commanded. "I'm still your mother and I want answers."

Disbelief ruled his features, "You've all lost your minds since I've been gone. Since when do we tell the family –"

"Ennis, calm down," Savannah called in a composed, pleasant manner. At least she prayed it sounded composed and pleasant because she didn't feel either at the moment. "We'll work this out."

Monty puffed his lower lip, "It's my fault. I told them."

It was a rare occasion when someone rendered Savannah speechless. With those words, Monty not only succeeded in stealing verbal communication from her but he also robbed her next breath. She sat, visibly stunned. Firstly, she couldn't imagine the degree of outrage flowing through the family. Mostly, she couldn't bear the thought of the young boy knowing that particular fact of life at such an early age.

Both hers and Ennis's heads spun to face little Monty, fright prominent in their features. Savannah could literally feel the blood sinking to her toes, "Monty?" Then she forced herself to ask, "When did you find out?"

"Yesterday. When you and Uncle Ennis were together."

Of course it was yesterday, she furiously berated herself. *It was the first and only time you lost all rational thought and flagrantly caved to your primal desires. All with blatant disregard to any repercussions your decision might have. Way to go, stupid.*

"Don't you remember?" Monty continued, "You said it."

The boy specifically said she'd "said it" but what was "it"? *Okay, something isn't geeing and hawing...* "What did I say, Monty?"

The little boy closed his eyes, mentally referring to the time, "You said, 'We'll find a way to tell them we're not 'gaged.' I heard it when you was holding me."

Once the information mulled around between her ears, Savannah started to smile. The tension eased, allowing her to think about something else besides making a quick escape. She and Ennis drew long, deep breaths that attracted the family's attention. Savannah didn't really care at that point.

"Ennis," Cal summoned, "you just spent another night alone with a woman you're not *'gaged* to."

"I was gonna ask," Dane played off the comment. "What'd you

two do last night to keep busy? Play poker?"

"Yeah," Jake snickered, "*strip* poker."

Savannah felt Ennis jerk and immediately Jake jumped like he'd been bitten, "Damn, Ennis." He rubbed his leg, "I was only kidding."

Jake might have been kidding but Savannah's cheeks glowed red with embarrassment. Ennis saw it and his hand covered hers resting on her knee.

Dane leaned back in his chair, observing their reactions to the bantering. Savannah caught his line of vision and looked away. From the corner of her eye she saw him smile. He rose, making a beeline to her chair. She felt her heart shift into overdrive with sincere alarm that he'd blurt something hurtful. He leaned down, whispering, "Ennis found that box of necessities, didn't he?"

She cut her vision to him, silently pleading with him to keep quiet. Dane patted her back, "Your secret is safe with me, Peach."

She highly doubted it. One thing about Ennis's brothers – they loved aggravating him to an unmerciful degree. She couldn't think of anything juicier to pester him with except this. She supposed brothers tormented each other to a certain extent, like a rite of passage of sorts. The Rutherford brothers, however, surpassed teasing and verged on vicious.

"What did you think we were talking about?" Bobbi inquired in a straightforward manner while rearranging the eggs on her plate with her fork.

Savannah prayed for something or someone to rescue them from the scrutiny – a phone call, a power outage, anything, because the Avon lady sure couldn't plow the snow outside and neither could an encyclopedia salesman.

"Mama," Ennis tried to redirect the conversation, "I never said we were engaged. Everyone else twisted it into wedding bells with me bringing her here."

"Not true," Cal zeroed in on Savannah while chewing a piece of bacon. He spoke to his brother without breaking visual contact with the red-faced female in question, "I specifically remember talking to you not long ago. You said, and I quote, 'I'll marry this girl if it's the last thing I do.'"

Ennis blinked slowly. Savannah sensed he ran a plethora of scenarios through his mind, all more painful than the last, all in store for his oldest brother. She felt bad for her partner. His family was worse than hers in some ways. Her family outright shot at each other while his delighted in pecking at him. While marriage ranked last in her goals in life, she still smarted that Cal embarrassed his brother so. Every one of his siblings were menaces, she'd decided, just on varying levels.

"I did say that," Ennis admitted without daring to look in her general direction. His temper simmered with every word, "But number one, I realize how she feels about marriage at this point and number two, I said that in strict confidence."

Bobbi unleashed a boisterous laugh, startling everyone present, including Savannah. The entire brood focused on the sister-in-law who, after a short time, gathered her decorum, "Ennis, honey, you know there's no such thing in this family."

"No sh –" Ennis caught himself before blurting his original

thought. "No kidding." He put a hand to Savannah's shoulder, "Let's go, sugar."

"Go where?" she asked with a thin veil of incredulity. "There's fifteen feet of snow out there, plus your family wants answers. Let's hash it out now so we can eat." Avoiding the subject created the mess in the first place. Doing so now only served to frustrate and anger the family since they wanted an explanation. Frankly, Savannah thought they deserved answers. She felt lower than a snake for allowing the misinformation to circulate through the family and community. She and Ennis committed a lie of omission that ballooned into a veritable nightmare. Unpleasant as it was, one of them needed to grow up and explain. Judging by his expression, Ennis still voted to pout so Savannah decided to tackle the truth, "Ennis and I do share strong feelings for each other but getting married isn't in my immediate future."

Their faces fell with disappointment in one form or another and like a passenger on a sinking ship, she scrambled for a lifeboat, "But if it was, I'd look to him for it. We've known each other a year so we don't take our relationship lightly." She met every face in the crowd, ensuring the gravity of her words hit, "We depend on each other every day. We trust each other with our lives. That itself counts for plenty." She lifted Ennis's hand from her shoulder and held it, "I don't know what I'd do without him."

"The same goes for me," the calm finally returned to Ennis's voice. He hugged her close against him. Savannah enjoyed the feeling of it. Lately though, she liked everything about Ennis, even his incessant snoring. That concerned her too. When a man's ripsaw snoring sounded "cute" to her, it was time for a shrink or a preacher but she was so out of sorts, she doubted either could cure her now.

She looked at her plate like a famished lion, "I really hope that answers your questions because I'm starving."

The group's attention glued to her then finally subdued smiles sprouted from most. Cal spoke first, "It's good enough for me."

Jake waited for his oldest brother to chance the first bite without further confrontation then shoveled into his own food. Dane released a long sigh, patted Savannah's back again then sat down, "Don't know about the rest of you but I think we've got a wildcat aboard our family tree." He winked at her, "Unofficially, of course."

Bobbi made eye contact with Savannah. With a smile, she gave the "unofficial family member" a wink and a nod. Savannah still sweated Mama Rutherford's reaction. History predicted if trouble lurked anywhere it was on Savannah Prince's tongue. If the older woman took her speech the wrong way, it didn't matter how the others felt.

Mama studied her though not in a judging way. She looked up at Ennis who still hugged Savannah close, their fingers still intertwined. Mama broke a grin that paled in comparison to the others, "Welcome to the family, Savannah. Unofficially, of course. But anytime you want to make it official, we're all expecting invitations."

Savannah finally relaxed, "And I promise to send them Overnight Express."

14

After the unnerving scene at breakfast, Savannah desperately needed time to gather her wits. She ate well as did everyone once the situation had been explained but what she craved was a few minutes alone. Once the breakfast dishes were washed and dried, she planned to migrate to a quiet corner and just breathe.

While Mama washed the dishes, Savannah, along with Bobbi, dried them. The latter took time out to put Monty down for a nap. She hadn't been gone very long when Savannah caught movement from the corner of her eye. Glancing up, she witnessed Bobbi covertly leaning toward the living room entry where the men congregated after the meal. *Sneaky*, thought the detective. Savannah heard the deep laughter of the men then a quieter span of time passed. It reminded Savannah of kids playing. A quiet stretch almost always followed rowdy laughter.

She returned to her duties while Bobbi remained engrossed in eavesdropping. Savannah carefully wiped the plates with a dishcloth. Mama's china was an older pattern of delicate pink roses that lined the plate's edge. The china showed signs of diligent use with the pattern fading or wearing in places along with a chip here and there. Grandma

Culberson's china looked similar to Mama's. The plates saw many meals and fed many mouths.

"You might want to break up the party in the living room."

Although the words were whispered in her ear, Savannah jumped like someone screamed. Bobbi apologized, "When I put Monty to bed for a nap, I overheard the gist of their conversation. They're trying to pry out of Ennis if you and he, you know, last night."

"I see," she said, tabling what she originally intended to say. "*Oh shit*" just had a way of offending people sometimes, plus it gave away the secret pretty damn quick. Her partner's steel resolve never wavered at work. Around enough testosterone, however, any red-blooded male might cave. Savannah suspected Ennis aspired to impress his brothers his whole life – but if he disclosed their intimate activities, it would be to crush whatever feelings he thought Dane had for her. "What did Ennis say?"

Clearly uncomfortable with the subject, Bobbi stressed, "He's staying firm for now but if he's a typical Rutherford, his ego will turn loose of the truth or a creative lie, whichever serves the purpose."

Even with her limited experience with brothers, Savannah knew Bobbi was right. The truth or a creative lie went for most of the male gender when trying to impress other men. Now she was grateful to Cal's wife for being so nosy.

She wiped her hands on the dishcloth then offered it to Bobbi, "I'm going to go remove temptation."

Bobbi gladly took the dishcloth, suggesting, "And toss his brothers in the snow while you're at it."

Savannah padded quietly over the caramel colored carpet toward the living room. Learning from Bobbi's tactics, she stayed to the side of the door and tilted her ear to the room. The men's voices remained low and secretive as they spoke. She heard Cal first, "So what if you did it? It's not like her daddy will come here with a shotgun."

"Actually, that would be a valid concern," Ennis responded. "You haven't met her father."

Dane was next, "How can you sleep in the same county with that woman without jumping in the saddle? Man, she's hot." He waited only a moment for a reply then, "Damn Ennis, I left you a box of condoms. Do I have to draw you a picture on how to use them too?"

She nearly laughed but a scuffle and Cal's authoratative tone stopped her, "Ennis, sit down. He's just being stupid."

Ennis's tone wiped the smile off her face, "You shut up about her. *She's not interested.*" He sounded threatening even to her and after last night, she'd probably pounce on Georgia or Seth if they teased her too hard about him as well.

A rising "ooh" came from the group of men. With a jovial chuckle Jake accused, "Yeah, they did it. You both looked disheveled this morning."

"And a little too happy," Cal added.

Jake blatantly baited Ennis with his comment, she hoped her partner understood that. Both she and Ennis showered and fixed up before venturing out that morning and if they appeared disheveled, the wind was to blame. And if they looked happy as Cal said, well, they *were.*

"Where the hell did you learn a word like disheveled?" Ennis wanted to know.

"Geez, Ennis. I *is* a high school graduate."

Figuring it was time to save Ennis from slaying his brothers – or vice versa – Savannah chose that moment to walk in, "Hi guys. Whatcha talkin' about?" Besides the room falling deathly quiet, the bug-eyed stares she received rated up there with "priceless". She joined Ennis on the loveseat and snuggled in close with her hand resting on his thigh. Her partner swallowed hard. Every male in the room focused on the location of her hand.

"Nothin'," Dane offered in a choked voice.

"I didn't intend to interrupt your conversation," she stated almost apologetically while the tip of her finger began leisurely tracing circles on Ennis's leg.

Dane's vision riveted on the motion of her hand, "Honey, you don't merely interrupt, you're a bona fide show stopper in all fifty states."

Even as Cal warned Dane to shut up, she felt Ennis's leg tense beneath her hand. Indeed, his whole body grew taut with anger, his narrowed vision aimed directly at Dane.

Savannah tried to alleviate the situation, "Don't mind me. Go 'head with what you were saying."

Jake cleared his throat nervously, looked away, "Our conversation wasn't exactly meant for womenfolk."

"We were discussing the fairer sex," Cal confessed as he rose from his seat. "And I think we've exhausted the subject."

"You can never exhaust that subject," Dane argued, "especially talkin' about women like Peach."

Savannah saw Ennis roll his fist. She couldn't have him launching himself at his brother in an all-out brawl. Firstly, there was a blizzard outside. Secondly, she wasn't sure if the two could be separated before blood was spilled.

From the corner of her eye, she watched Cal smack Dane in the head with his cowboy hat and heard a solid "shut the hell up" from the eldest. From Ennis, she felt the heat of his temper rising. His mouth opened to lash Dane and Savannah did the only thing that came to mind. She cupped Ennis's face in her palms and planted a slow and – hopefully – memorable kiss on him. Ennis's lips, pursed in anger, finally relaxed as the kiss continued. Savannah felt his strong fingers stroke her arm then travel down until curling around her hand, holding it.

A subdued whistle upped the ante in Dane's annoying campaign, "Hey, little brother. Before you two steam the windows, remember you're in Ma and Pa's place."

Ennis's grasp instinctively tightened on her arm. He attempted – though not earnestly – to separate from the kiss. Savannah took that moment to caress behind his ear with her fingertips. During their frolicking the night before, she learned it brought a smile when she did it. Today she merely meant to stop a killing.

She saw Ennis open his eyes to stare a blazing hole through Dane. The kiss wasn't inappropriate by any means. It lasted longer than most friendly kisses however most women weren't put between two brothers who enjoyed pestering each other.

"Y'know, Dane," Cal mentioned, "a woman can only contain a

man's anger so long. You keep peckin' at Ennis and we're liable to find you stickin' out of a snow bank later on."

"He's about to throw her aside and strangle you," Jake agreed.

It shocked Savannah when Ennis ripped away from the kiss. She automatically held him to prevent him from following through on Jake's words. As another surprise, Ennis's fingers glided up her arm to touch her cheek. "Let's get out of here," he whispered.

Savannah ventured a smile. When his features relaxes, she leaned in to whisper what Ennis would describe as a "sweet nothing". His "sweet nothings" ended up being the most sensual words she'd ever heard from a man. Words that forced any sensible woman to listen to and comply with – so he could make good on his promise. Now it was her turn. Her "sweet nothings" consisted of one sentence, brief but vivid.

Judging by the brother's expectant, wide-eyed gazes, she could have told Ennis they were going outside to build a snowman and they'd have put their own raunchy spin on it.

Ennis's eyes sprang open and he struggled to a standing position, her hand in his, "We gotta go."

Savannah winked at the brothers, "I think he means it."

Ennis cupped his hand around her ear, whispering back, "If you're still conscious after I'm finished with you, *then* you can do what you said."

Bobbi stepped in, amazed at the silence in the room and quite astonished at the men's expressions. She looked to Savannah for an answer, "What are y'all doing?"

Savannah's blue eyes followed the room, momentarily stopping on each brother, "Oh," she replied with a grin, "nothin'."

15

They retired to the ranch house and immediately after shedding her coat, Savannah found herself pressed against the wall, Ennis's body aligning with hers, his erection pressing against her belly while his lips recapturing hers in a fiery, demanding kiss.

Showing her strong-willed side lost its appeal lately. The longer they were together, the more her heart trusted him and the more her brain accepted that Ennis loved her for the right reasons. Keeping her guard up twenty four hours a day got old quick but it also constructed a formidable obstacle regarding relationships until now. It felt damn good to wholly trust a man.

She curled her arms around Ennis's neck, moaning as his hand slipped beneath her shirt and tenderly palmed her breast. He briefly separated from the kiss whispering, "I can't wait to get these clothes off you." To emphasize his point, he stroked her nipple through the bra while diving in for another kiss – then destiny struck again...

A knock on the door brought a frustrated groan from Ennis and as they parted from the kiss, an exasperated sigh escaped Savannah's lips. Long past losing her temper, she resigned herself to savoring the sweetness of his kiss, the memory of his touch. In the back of her mind she expected an interruption of some variety, whether it be the phone, the door or visit from a celestial being, she *knew* it would happen.

Unfortunately, Ennis fired mad instantly. He flushed crimson and the muscles in his jaw clenched and released. She patted his chest, trying to calm him, "It's okay. It's not the only opportunity we'll have."

He pressed a kiss to her forehead, "We'll have to go back to Atlanta just for privacy. Your family isn't nearly this intrusive."

She returned the kiss with one to his chin, "That's because they don't live close by and they realize they risk grievous bodily harm if they show up uninvited. Besides my temper, that's a trait I inherited from my father. I hate having impromptu visitors. So, in a way, you can thank him for our privacy at home."

Ennis cocked a brow, "I would but I don't think he likes me all that much."

The visitor knocked again, this time five times instead of the initial three. Ennis reached beside Savannah and yanked the door open. Savannah noticed he scarcely attempted to hide his aggravation as Dane poked his head in. Seeing her basically flat against the wall telegraphed to the brother he'd interrupted at a most inopportune time. "Sorry to barge in," he apologized.

Ennis took her hand and they both roosted on the side of the bed. Still plenty mad, he blatantly hinted, "You can barge out anytime."

Dane closed the door behind him. Savannah realized his expression didn't indicate secret pleasure that he'd disturbed them. It indicated something wrong.

He removed his hat, seemingly unsure of how to begin the conversation. Savannah hadn't seen Dane so ill at ease since she'd been there. She watched him dig in his jeans pocket. From it he retrieved her cell phone, handed it to her, "You left this at the house. Your sister called and I took the liberty of answering. She was crying pretty good but dried up as soon as she realized it wasn't you on the phone."

Alarm brought Savannah to her feet. Whatever troubled Georgia the past several days evidently broke loose that morning – and it absolutely figured that Savannah would be a zillion miles away, unable to help. Her sister rarely cried and considering Dane's apprehensive demeanor, she'd been close to hysterical.

She flipped open the phone while asking details of the call. Dane withdrew, shying away from the inquiry. He shifted his vision to Ennis, "She kinda let the cat out of the bag before she knew it wasn't you. She said Matthew filed for divorce."

The anger boiling inside her percolated to the surface, "That bastard. I knew he'd hurt her. *I knew it.*" Before she punched in Georgia's number, Dane put a hand to her wrist, "Peach, I'm no expert on relationships but I'd keep that bit of info to myself. She already feels lousy."

Normally, being lectured set her temper ablaze. This time, she hesitated before completing the call and contemplated Dane's advice. He was highly uncomfortable discussing Georgia's plight. He shifted his weight from one foot to the other, and refused to look Savannah in the eyes more often than not. After a moment, she realized he had a valid point. Georgia was miserable enough.

"You're right," she replied genuinely. "I'm afraid my feelings for Matthew aren't the warmest and I don't want to upset her anymore than she already is." She finished dialing and waited...

Ennis remained seated on the bed. The news of the divorce sucked the air from him. He never met Matthew but only saw pictures of him. Georgia spoke proudly of her husband and displayed pictures of him throughout her house. She faithfully wrote him, keeping him apprised of news from home. When she visited with him on the phone, she reminded Ennis of an infatuated teenager. If anyone was madly in love, it was her.

Before Ennis left for Texas, she mentioned Matthew scheduled a trip home for Christmas. Instead, the rat bastard served her divorce papers as a gift. Ennis could only imagine her devastation upon receiving them. Now *he* wanted to kill Matthew too. Georgia possessed a kind, loving heart. She was a trusting soul. Ennis feared this divorce would change her like all divorces changed people, making them unwilling to share their heart with another for a long time, if ever again. She didn't deserve that.

Savannah passed the pleasantries of greetings and broached the difficult subject. Ennis heard Georgia weeping over the phone and he winced at the sorrowful sound. Savannah worked to calm her down, using a gentle even tone for her supportive words.

Like his brother, Ennis grew antsy and decided to leave his partner in peace. He and Dane met in the kitchen. Ennis began brewing coffee for them as his brother whispered to him, "That girl sounds just like Peach. Well, with the distinct exception of the crying…"

"Cut it out," Ennis warned while checking Savannah's facial expression. She successfully concealed the anger in her voice, not in her features. She was about to explode with rage, Ennis sensed it. The instant she glanced in his general direction, he busied himself tending to the coffee pot. He took great pains to look busy, not nosy.

"I'm making an observation is all," Dane said. "Can't I do that?"

"No," Ennis mumbled back.

Dane leaned with his back against the cabinet, crossed his arms over his chest, "Ennis, for weeks I've heard about Georgia and her cooking rival's a chef. Not even Mama can make cookies that melt in your mouth like that. This woman is a complete mystery and you're telling me I can't inquire about her?"

"That's precisely what I'm telling you." He watched the coffee drip sluggishly into the carafe at first then pick up momentum. He intended to snag the first cup just for something to do. He'd pour the second cup for Savannah and if Dane didn't shut up about Georgia, his dear brother wouldn't be around to consume anything short of Ennis's fist.

Dane lowered his voice, "Does she look like Peach too? Just answer that."

"I'm gonna slug you if you don't button it. Stay away from Georgia." His voice carried further than he expected and Savannah's vision redirected to the men. From his viewpoint, she wasn't upset or happy about the outburst. Perhaps she hadn't heard him clearly – he hoped.

Ennis didn't wait for the first cup to brew. He jerked the carafe out and poured what amounted to half a cup then replaced the decanter. After blowing the steam off, he sipped the hot, stout liquid. Keeping a cautious eye toward Savannah, he whispered, "You'd be surprised at how *not* alike they are. Leave her alone until this shit is sorted out."

It was Dane's turn to fly mad, "Geez, Ennis, I'm not a clod. I may not know her but I ain't stupid enough to go intrude on her right now. I'm asking questions is all."

Ennis flinched and not due to the sting of hot coffee on his tongue. Savannah heard that outburst loud and clear. He couldn't bear to measure her expression now so he turned away. She'd be madder than a wet cat when she hung up. The thought of it positively deflated him and he leaned against the kitchen cabinet to peer out the window. She would think Dane was after her sister in her most vulnerable state – hell, that's what *he* thought too. He grew up with Dane, he knew him like a book.

Dane clearly didn't know when to quit, "She got a favorite flower?"

Ennis took a calming breath. It failed miserably, "I couldn't say. I'm more interested in her sister." He heard her end the conversation with Georgia and click off the phone. Here it came... The storm from hell. All because Dane wouldn't mind his own business.

He heard her on the phone again, this time scheduling a flight to Atlanta that day. It didn't surprise him she'd go back as soon as possible. Georgia needed her support and being a loving sister, Savannah would provide it.

A few moments later he noticed the silence behind him. Suddenly her voice sounded so close it startled him, "Here's a picture of Georgia." She'd stated it matter-of-factly. Ennis attempted to gauge whether that was a good or bad thing.

He wheeled to see her hand a photo to Dane. His brother, as expected, warmed all over at the sight, "She's a mighty beautiful lady. Thanks for the looksee, Peach."

No doubt that "looksee" would last Dane through the cold nights as he daydreamed about how to contact her and when. The fact that Savannah showed him a picture bowled Ennis over completely. She was very protective of her sister and Ennis feared she just fed Georgia to a wolf.

She replaced the photo in her purse with a firm request, "Dane, I know she's a knockout. She's also got a heart of gold but she tends to trust the wrong people sometimes. That's what happened with Matthew. She needs a kind heart to complement hers and someone to love her, really love her for who she is. If you're serious about seeing her, I'd appreciate it if you'd give her some space right now. Let the shock wear off. I know Ennis has warned you but all I'm doing is asking you to wait a while."

Dane listened to every word and upon completion of her speech, he nodded, "I promise. In fact, I'll run my impending visit past you, not my brother. Ennis seems to think I eat women for lunch."

"Devour them whole then spit out the remains like an owl, yes," Ennis agreed. He defended himself against the wide-eyed stares of his companions. "Remember Lily?"

"Geez, Ennis, I was in sixth grade. So what I kissed your sweetheart and took her to the monkey bars at recess a few times? I didn't know we were holding grudges like the Hatfields and McCoys. Are we gonna fight about this when we're in the rest home too?"

Since Dane so poetically dissected it, the absurdity of the argument embarrassed him. Lily was merely the first girl Dane swiped from him. Dane left Jenny Lee alone, of course, probably sensing that her elevator didn't go to the top but practically every other girl was fair game. Savannah didn't know that. All she heard was the bickering over a grade school crush.

Ennis couldn't look at Savannah. He already saw the smile curving her mouth. "It's just the point," he said. "If you'll do it then you'll do it now."

"I think Georgia's probably outgrown the monkey bars by now and you've already put your stamp on Savannah."

The overwhelming urge to deck his brother needled Ennis. His hands literally itched to punch him. He stared at Dane with near disbelief as the older Rutherford dared him to deny it in front of Savannah. On the other hand, she stood, volleying her vision between the two then settled on Ennis with expectation of an answer.

Why the hell not, he figured. "You're damn right I have and you'd best stay your distance."

"Boys," she summoned, almost smiling at Ennis's response. "Don't argue. I'd hate to break up a brawl before I leave."

Just the sound of her sultry accent calmed Ennis, "He's not worth bruising my hand. So when is your flight?"

"I leave in four hours."

"What?" The word shot from both men like a misfired weapon. Neither could believe what they heard. Suddenly quarrelling over women took a back seat. "Four hours?" Ennis basically stammered. "But that hardly gives us any time..." Then he realized how he sounded, "I know Georgia needs you but I'm gonna miss you."

Savannah stepped closer and lifted to tiptoe. She tenderly kissed him, whispering, "I'll miss you too."

Dane cleared his throat, "I'll vacate so you can pack." He gave her a peck on the cheek, "Thanks for having an open mind about me meeting Georgia. S'more than I can say for my own brother."

Ennis wrapped his arm around Savannah's waist, brought her close. He spoke for her, "Get out before I change her mind."

Dane slipped his hat on again and eased out the door, leaving them alone. Ennis felt her settle in his embrace, her head resting against his heart. He did not resist the temptation to stroke her long hair. In fact he luxuriated in it, "Speaking of that, why do you think it's a good idea?"

Savannah wrapped him in her own embrace, "I don't right now but Georgia wanted to know who answered the phone. Evidently she and Dane talked a few minutes and he calmed her down pretty well. She wants to meet him too."

Ennis couldn't believe his ears. Dane successfully calmed a hysterical woman without firing her temper? Usually he'd veer into taboo territory and the female threatened to slap him so hard his nose hair would fly out. But Georgia *liked* Dane? Obviously this needed more investigation. "How was she?" he asked.

"Found out that's why she was depressed earlier when we spoke. She'd had the divorce papers a week. She called Seth and Leah and some of her friends and they gave her support then Daddy found out somehow. That's the reason for her meltdown today. Daddy told her from far back how lousy Matthew was." She pulled back temporarily, "I swear, Ennis, if I ever get married, he's not invited to the wedding." Then she hugged him tighter.

Ennis returned the firm embrace, "Now don't go makin' judgments in haste. He may change with time."

She parted slightly from him, her reply stern, "He's not invited, *period.*"

"Okay, he's not invited." He bobbed his brow, "So when's our big day?"

The question brought a genuine relaxed smile, "Nice try, sonny."

"Call me that again and I swear I'll label you a dame."

Savannah lifted to tiptoe and pecked a kiss on his lips, "Truce then."

Ennis expected her to break away and begin the unpleasant task of packing. Instead she gazed wistfully – what he hoped was wistfully – at him. His brain screamed for him to ask her thoughts, his gut told him to shut up and enjoy. He listened to his gut. A brief moment later, he applauded his decision as she wrapped him in another strong embrace and rested her cheek against his heart. Delightfully startled, Ennis returned the gesture. His daddy told him the best feeling in the world was holding the woman you loved. Ennis always prided himself on his father's wisdom.

"I love you."

It was hushed, so hushed he barely perceived the words. His heart, though, caught every syllable. It sped in his chest, pounding a brisk rhythm in her ear though she showed no sign of noticing. Ennis noticed big time. His head grew swimmy and his knees got weak. Savannah said she loved him. She actually said it!

Mere mortals could not restrain a momentous reaction yet Ennis forced himself to restrain the impulse of hoisting her in his arms, throwing her on the bed and repeatedly ravishing her from head to toe. Ennis rode out the urge and settled for closing his embrace a bit more, "I love you too."

The time constraint demanded she start packing but withdrawing from Ennis's embrace produced an abysmal loneliness inside her. It had been many years since an acute sadness rooted so deep. What started as a vacation ended with gaining a new family. Instead of one brother, she added Cal, Jake and Dane to her list. And Bobbi acted like a sister to her, and she claimed little Monty as another nephew. Most importantly, Savannah gained a mother figure in Mama Rutherford. To her surprise, the two got along famously, despite the fact both admitted their noggins were made of marble. Savannah assumed they'd clash like oil and water but the exact opposite occurred. Ennis's entire family accepted her wholly as he had, quirks and all. Going home meant leaving one home for another now.   With that, another distressing quandary presented itself. She couldn't very well walk into Georgia's house and announce she was deliriously in love with Ennis while her older sister battled the pain of divorce. As profound as her joy was, it had to take a back seat until she settled Georgia down and got her started on a new life without Matthew.

The image of Dane peeked into her mind. Now there was a high caliber, bona fide scalawag if she ever saw one but he possessed a good heart like Ennis. He, like Ennis, also lifted a dreary mood or bad one by merely cracking a silly joke. He entertained her with a simple facial expression, and could probably tell entire stories without uttering a word. His actions with Monty's situation and demeanor moments earlier told volumes about his true personality and maturity.

A tiny grin played at her mouth. Dane Rutherford might be the best medicine for her sister – after a point. She'd make sure they met and she'd make sure to wring his neck if he hurt Georgia in any respect.

16

Two Months Later

It should have been illegal to be that happy. If lawmakers in Washington ever discovered how love changed people into smiling idiots, they'd either tax it or declare it criminal. Savannah decided whatever the fine, it was worth the price. Love was a potent drug and whether the dose was infinitesimal or humongous, the result remained the same. She laughed more, smiled practically all the time and felt positively lost without Ennis Rutherford.

Savannah expected him to mention the scars on her back each day that passed but he didn't. Instead he chose to respect her privacy. He wanted to ask, she knew that. Every night when they retired to bed he stroked along the lengths of several scars and she sensed him staring at them when she undressed. Someday she would explain the joys of living with a brutal drunken father. Ennis knew very little about her childhood, only that R.J. was an abusive drunk, not that her father reached a degree of rage that could make Satan recoil.

Contrary to her partner, Savannah found her siblings burrowing into her private life the way gophers dig their holes. Every so often their questioning verged on the intensity of the Spanish Inquisition. Consequently when Georgia ran out of steam, Seth seized control, whipping out questions at a rate that gave her the jitters. She understood Georgia's curiosity but Seth? The man hardly recognized love when it sideswiped *him*, how could he spot anyone else suffering a direct hit from Cupid's arrow?

Savannah had returned home expecting to find her sister dissolved in tears because of the divorce. Georgia was but Savannah soon discovered her sister found a new friend in Dane. While Savannah traversed the country at forty thousand feet, Dane called Georgia "to keep her company until the plane arrived". At first it peeved the youngest Prince however once she noticed Georgia's voice settle upon mentioning Dane, Savannah's anger subsided. He tried to help in his own way but as long as he kept his distance for a while, she'd be okay with him. Georgia needed time to heal from the initial blow of Matthew's betrayal. Rebound romance almost always failed and Dane didn't want to see Savannah's temper, she was quite positive of it.

Another thing she was positive of – she never should have agreed to play dominos with Ennis Rutherford. Forget the fact she played the game as competently as she bowled. She was more a chess person than bowler – and quite obviously her skill lacked in the domino department as well. Ennis promised to teach her the rules, help her finesse her game for when they played against his family. He swore they drew blood with each game. Personally, she considered his method of play just as lethal. He accumulated points at an alarming rate – almost as alarming as she lost points. Something was wrong, she thought. No one could suck that bad at any game.

Their shift was an hour over and she'd planned to head home and relax until Ennis had the bright idea of playing a "friendly" game of dominos. That friendly game quickly demolished what remained of a perfectly good mood. Her normally mild-mannered partner evolved into a creature she hardly recognized as he greedily counted up tiles like Midas counting money. She'd bet real money that he rewrote a few rules in his favor…

They sat at her desk, Ennis across from her, taking turns placing dominos in a snakelike form around her desktop. Savannah never felt so dumb in her life. Every time she placed a tile against his, Ennis playfully swatted it away, "Won't work. Try another." He repeated the phrase so often she expected to hear those exact words in her dreams that night. Considering she never played the game, she thought her progress equaled novice, not turnip.

They agreed to play until one player reached one hundred points, whatever that meant. At the meager rate she collected points, she estimated approximately twenty years – that's how long it would take for her to win the game.

Ennis attempted, though not very hard, to explain the game to her. She just assumed he wanted revenge for their last poker game she won. She learned her partner accepted defeat like winning a trip to the dentist.

Ennis placed a tile next to hers and declared himself the winner. Studying the maze of dominos before her, she frowned, "How do you know you won?" Before giving him time to answer, she threw her hands skyward in defeat, "I surrender. Considering all the rules, chemistry is easier than dominos."

"You just need practice," Ennis assured with more glee than she thought necessary.

"No," another voice interjected, "she just needs to realize you're cheatin'."

Savannah recognized Dane's drawl instantly. She looked up at the same time Ennis glanced behind him. Dane stood in his usual attire of jeans, boots and cowboy hat, and today, a blue plaid shirt showcased his broad chest. He gifted Savannah with a classic Dane smile – ample and easy with a flavor of mischievousness thrown in for good measure.

She returned his smile with one of her own. "What're you doing here?" she asked, rounding her desk to grab him in a hug.

"Yeah," Ennis finally rose to face his brother, accusing, "what *are* you doing here?"

Dane squeezed Savannah tight, "Thanks for the warm welcome, Peach. My brother's forgotten his upbringin'."

"No, I haven't, and I ain't forgot why you wanted to come to Atlanta."

Ennis's statement rang true. It also reminded her Dane promised to ask her before making the trip to meet Georgia. Her partner stood, hands on hips, waiting for an explanation. Frankly, she wanted one too. Dane, however, wouldn't stop hugging on her like keeping her occupied might prevent her from mentioning that fact – which, of course, it wouldn't.

Ennis simmered while Dane enveloped Savannah in a bear hug. His brow sank faster than a stone in water, "Mind letting her go? Her eyes are bugging."

Officers and detectives walking past stared at the two locked in the embrace and frankly, it irritated Ennis.

He dreaded fielding subsequent questions about the scene so breaking it up seemed sensible enough. After all, most of their colleagues suspected Ennis and Savannah were an item. The two never confirmed or denied their relationship for professional reasons but Ennis knew they weren't stupid. Now, with another man hanging on Savannah, eyebrows would surely raise and tongues would wag.

To expedite his wishes, Ennis stepped closer, "People are staring."

Reluctantly, his older brother released her. And as he no doubt feared, she reminded Dane of his promise. Ennis was grateful she mentioned it. It sounded far nicer than his intended approach.

Dane's vision shifted from Ennis back to her, "I know I said I'd call. But –"

"But I didn't think my little sister should screen my visitors," Georgia offered as she stepped into the office. "You can blame me."

It took a lot to render Savannah speechless. Ennis glanced her way, seeing her mouth partially open to speak but nothing emerged. The image clearly amused Georgia, "Thank you for looking out for me, though. Thank you both."

Ennis responded with a subtle nod. Savannah still searched for a reply. Her sister decided to clarify the details, "Dane and I have spoken on the phone several times and I wanted to see him. I invited him for a visit and he warned me that you both might tar and feather him if he showed without advance notice. That's why we're here."

"To save him from a killin'?" Ennis finally spoke.

"Something like that," was her answer.

Dane rounded Savannah's desk while addressing his brother, "I told Georgia you'd chase me out of town. I also said Savannah was the only one with a heart." He studied the dominos arranged on her desk, "You know, cheatin' on your girlfriend is a crime. Cheatin' on your girlfriend at dominos is inexcusable." He leveled a look on Ennis, "What kind of scam are you pullin', brother?"

"Shut up," Ennis warned then shied away from Savannah's judging frown. She joined Dane at the desk where he pointed to three of Ennis's dominos, "These aren't legal, at least with the rules *we* grew up with." He examined the tiles still left in her reserve. Methodically, he pointed to four possibilities, "These woulda worked. 'Course he probably woulda lost."

"Snitch," Ennis mumbled.

Savannah crossed her arms, her expression feigned annoyance, "I'll remember this, Ennis."

Georgia agreed, "I'm afraid she's got a good memory."

Dane slid his arm around Savannah's shoulders, "Let's all head to Georgia's and I'll introduce you girls to the real game of dominos. It's clear my brother needs a refresher course."

Savannah slanted her sister an inquiring look, "We won't be

intruding? After all, you two have wanted to meet for a while." A genuine smile crossed Georgia's features which brought one to her face as well.

"We'll have plenty of time together," the older sister assured. "We've been talking for months remember. We just thought now was a good time to see each other."

Ennis cleared his throat, still not happy about the situation, "Georgia, take things slow with him. He's faster than he looks."

Georgia laughed. The sound nearly brought tears to Savannah's eyes. Her sister hadn't laughed so openly since the divorce papers arrived. The only time she saw an indisputable sparkle in her green eyes was speaking of Dane. His appearance only brightened Georgia's demeanor. Savannah slid her arm around Dane, "Let's go. I can't wait to learn the game of dominos. The real game, I mean."

Dane hugged her against him while fending off Ennis's narrow look, "Don't worry, little brother. I'm sure if she wins," he bobbed his brow, "she'll give *you* a nice prize."

Ennis glanced to his partner hopefully. She winked at him, "You know I will."

"Sometimes," Dane added with his own wink to Georgia, "losing has its advantages."

J.L. Lemon lives in Texas surrounded by a loving and supportive family, two adorable and devoted puppies, and hordes of garden gnomes.

Before 2002, J.L. Lemon wrote opinions and product reviews for an online consumer guide. When fellow reviewers cited the author's knack for humor, she decided to return to writing fiction. To date, she's published 6 books with 5 installments in the Savannah Stories. There are 3 more in the works. For more titles from J.L. Lemon, please visit:

www.geocities.com/upatmidnightpublishing
www.geocities.com/authorjllemon

Savannah and Ennis keep the author busy taking dictation and making plenty of suggestions about their future.

www.ingramcontent.com/pod-product-compliance
Lightning Source LLC
Chambersburg PA
CBHW051917240626
47153CB00004B/1262